The Night Heroes:

Cry From the Coal Mine

by
Dr. Bo Wagner

Word of His Mouth Publishers
Mooresboro, NC

All Scripture quotations are taken from the **King James Version** of the Bible.

ISBN: 978-0-9856042-3-3
Printed in the United States of America
© 2012 Dr. Bo Wagner (Robert Arthur Wagner)

Word of His Mouth Publishers
PO Box 256
Mooresboro, NC 28114
704-477-5439
www.wordofhismouth.com

Chapter One

Carrie was getting carsick, Aly was her usual bubbly self, and I was wondering if there was any flat spot in the mountains of West Virginia. My name is Kyle, and I am a PK, a preacher's kid. Specifically, I am an evangelist's kid. For those of you who have no idea what an evangelist is, or what it is like to be the kid of one, let me help you out. Most people have homes that they live in 51 weeks a year and then they go on vacation for a week. As an evangelist's family, we rarely ever see home. My dad will preach a week of meetings in one state and then we will load up and be on to the next state and the next meeting.

This means that we live out of suitcases many different weeks of the year. We sleep in hotels or guest rooms in churches, and those guest rooms are usually called Prophet's Chambers. All of this traveling means that we really look forward to our few weeks at home.

Our weeks at home are actually our vacation. Weird, huh! Our home is in a little town called Polkville, just outside of the mighty metropolis of Shelby, NC. Okay, that mighty metropolis part is actually just a joke. Shelby is a relatively small town. And Polkville? Well, Polkville is just a tiny dot on the map. A nice dot, but still a dot.

Anyway, when my dad is doing an evangelistic campaign, he will travel around from church to church with me, my two sisters, and my mom. He will preach a week or so for a church and then we will pack our bags and be on to the next church and the next meeting. I am only fourteen, my sisters are twelve and eleven, but all of us have already been in 39 of the 50 states. From what dad says, the other eleven are just around the corner.

So anyway, Carrie was getting carsick, Aly was her usual bubbly self, and I was wondering if there was any flat spot in the mountains of West Virginia. We were on our way to the little town of Boomer, just outside of the slightly less little town of Smithers, which is just outside the tiny bit bigger town of Montgomery. We were on our way to Boomer Baptist Church to preach for them, and the winding mountain roads were not something that we kids were used to. As we pulled past Smithers, the road wound upward towards Boomer, and we could hear the wail of a train off in the distance. Just inside the Boomer town limits was the sign for Boomer Baptist Church on the right. We turned off the main road and maybe fifty feet further came to a railroad track, which ran right in front of the church. On that track was a traaaaaaaaaaaaaaain. I say it that way because we counted 120 railroad cars being pulled by that locomotive! It ambled slowly by, clickety-clack, clickety-clack, clickety-clack. Ten minutes later it finally cleared the track, and we pulled across into the parking lot. Pastor Neeson met us there, he and my dad shook hands, and his wife was there to hug my mom and us kids.

It had been a long day of traveling to get to Boomer, and we were all dead tired. But we were also something else... hungry! But this is one of the best parts of being in an evangelist's family: everywhere you go, the dear ladies of the church are sure to have a meal ready for you. Chicken, corn, green beans, mashed potatoes, homemade biscuits, sweet tea, and of course, dessert! I have learned that banana pudding is one of the four basic food groups, and I'm perfectly fine with that.

We had supper there in the fellowship hall of the church and then it was time to get ready for service. The first night is always the hardest. We will drive all day, eat in a hurry, quickly get our suitcases inside, get everything ironed, and rush to service. Our family will usually sing a special song or two, the church may have their choir sing, they will take up a love-offering, and then my dad will preach. I love my dad's preaching. He is a really good preacher, at least I think so. I know he loves the Lord, I know he loves people, and I really know that he loves us. Especially my mom, whom he is always winking and smiling at.

Service went pretty well that first night, everyone laughed at my dad's corny jokes before the message, and they all seemed encouraged by what he preached. It was a message about Heaven, which is one of my dad's favorite subjects. He seems to like preaching on Heaven a lot more since Phillip died. Phillip was a nice young man from our church, and all of us miss him like crazy.

After service we all went down into Montgomery to the Dairy Queen. Church people are like that; they like each other so much that even after a service is over, they usually go somewhere to sit around and talk for a while. There will always be a whole lot of smiles and laughter when they do.

After a while, though, the girls were getting sleepy. Not me, I'm a boy; I don't get sleepy like they do. They may smack me when they read this, but they'll have to catch me first. So, since they were getting sleepy, we went on back to the Prophet's Chamber. Mom and dad got our sleeping arrangements set up; they were in one room, the girls and I were in the room beside them on sleeping pallets.

For most folks, sleeping in a strange new place would be hard. But when you do it most of the year, after a while you get used to it. So we settled down, took time to read our

Bibles, which we all love, and then Mom and Dad came in and prayed with us. They left the room, turning off the lights as they left, and we closed our eyes and adjusted to the new sounds around us. I could hear the air conditioner kicking in. I could hear a car or two going down the road headed in the direction of Smithers. I could hear crickets from somewhere outside. I could hear the sound of a train whistle. And then I heard the conductor of the train call out three names: "Kyle! Carrie! Aly!"

Chapter Two

I sat straight up in bed. I looked to my left, and Carrie was sitting straight up in bed too. Same for Aly on my right. Only none of us were in bed anymore. We were all sitting on the front porch of an old railroad depot, and the sun was just coming up over the mountain behind us. In front of us sat an old train, with smoke belching from the engine in the front. Past the train was a river, and on the other side of the river another track for trains, and just past that a very high mountain, meaning that we were in a deep valley. The conductor stood staring at us as if he expected us to do something. For our part, we were looking back and forth from each other, to him, to the train, to the river, and back to each other again, wondering which one of us was dreaming. Finally, the conductor spoke again. "Kyle, Carrie, Aly. Climb aboard; he needs your help."

7

It's hard to explain what we all felt right then. Talking about it later, it was like a mixture of being scared, being curious, and wanting to laugh at how silly it all seemed, yet being amazed at how real it all felt. We sat there unsure what to do, and then the conductor spoke again. "Warner Children, come aboard this train this instant. You are here for a reason, and the night is waning fast. You have only five nights here to help him, and every moment lost will make it that much harder to do so. Your mother and father have taught you to help those in need, and this boy's need is dire. So once again, please, come aboard."

"With all due respect, Sir," said my sister Carrie, "we don't know you, and we don't even know how we got here. The last thing I remember is going to sleep. It is now quite clearly *daytime*, and yet you just said that the *night* was waning fast. Are we dreaming?"

"You obviously listen very carefully, Young Lady, and you are very perceptive. That is one of the reasons you children have been summoned here tonight, or today, depending upon your perspective. To answer your question, yes, you are dreaming, but no, you are not dreaming like you might think. You will wake up in the morning in your beds in the guest room, and you will be rested from a night of sleep, but what is happening right now, here in this daytime, is very real. Every decision you make will have an impact, and precious lives are hanging in the balance. Now, please climb aboard; we are wasting very valuable time."

My sisters and I looked at each other, still a bit unsure. It was little Aly who finally settled the issue. "Look," she said, her hazel eyes peeping out from under blonde bangs, "what do we have to lose? If this isn't a dream, then we obviously are not where we should be, and maybe this train will take us back. But if it is a dream, then whatever we do, we'll eventually wake up anyway. But if the conductor is right and some little boy needs us, how could we ever live with ourselves if we don't help him?"

A moment later we were climbing aboard into the engine room with the conductor. He pulled the cord overhead and with a "Whoot! Whoot!" the train slowly began to move. Dozens of wooden box cars were behind us, loaded with coal, weighing the train down and making the start-up a slow process. Each chug of the wheels, though, brought a tiny bit more forward momentum, a tiny bit more speed. Within a few minutes we were moving on down the tracks pretty quick, looking out the front window at the beautiful scenery passing by. "This is called the New River," said the conductor, "and this area is called the New River Gorge. In your day, if you will travel up the road a ways from Boomer, heading toward Fayetteville, you will cross a huge bridge called the New River Bridge. It will cross the river just right around this bend and will be the highest arch bridge in the Western Hemisphere."

Looking a little bewildered Carrie asked, "Pardon me, Mr. Conductor, but what do you mean 'in your day?' Whose day are we in, exactly?"

Smiling he replied, "You are very perceptive once again; I can see why you three were chosen. Well, if you want to know 'whose' day it is, I guess I can put it this way. It is William Taft's day if you want to know who the President of the United States is; it is William Glasscock's day if you want to know who the governor of West Virginia is; and it is Jeremy Buchanan's day if you want to know who the owner of the Leeborough mine is. It is presently the year 1912, and there is a coal war brewing."

My sister Carrie has long black hair, dark brown eyes, and glasses. Behind those glasses her eyes had grown wide, and she was looking up at me. Normally we fight a lot, like typical brothers and sisters. But in times when things are uncertain, she will run to dad first, but if he is not there she leans on me. Looking into her eyes at that moment I could see just a little bit of fear. The conductor had turned his eyes to the tracks ahead, so I went to her and threw my arm around her shoulder.

"Sis," I said, "whatever happens, you just stay close to me. I'm not as strong as dad, but I'm stronger than any other fourteen year old you know. And besides, all three of us know Jesus well enough to know that He'll be there for us no matter what happens."

I wasn't bragging in what I said about myself. Dad made sure we kids worked hard since we were little, especially me. We chopped and carried wood together, we carried and hung sheet rock, we did construction at the church, whatever needed doing, he made sure I had a part in it. As a result, I wasn't like most teenage boys. They had strong thumbs from playing video games all day, but I had a broad chest and strong arms and legs. Dad said that I was going to be hard to handle when I grew up. I was determined to be hard to handle now.

I also meant every word I said about Jesus. All three of us kids had gotten saved within the last few years, and we all knew that we could trust Him. From what Mom and Dad told me, I knew that I had more reason to trust him than most anyone else.

When Mom and Dad had been married just a few years, she got pregnant with me. Like all expecting couples, the next few months were a whirlwind of nursery preparations, financial adjustments, and doctor's visits. It was on one of those doctor's visits that Mom and Dad's world fell in on them. The nurse technician was doing the ultrasound, and for some reason, she kept focusing it on my head. Dad said that he noticed right away that she kept on going back to a dark spot in my brain and digitally circling it.

Mom and Dad asked her what that spot was, but she simply said, "The doctor will go over the ultrasound with you shortly." Then, she left the room, taking a CD from the computer along with her.

Dad said the wait felt like an eternity, but they were finally summoned into the doctor's office. "Mr. and Mrs. Warner," he began, "there is a problem here that needs dealing with. Your son has a spot on his brain, an abscess really, and we need to send you to a specialist in Charlotte to have it checked out. I've already made you an appointment; it is for two weeks from today."

The next two weeks Mom and Dad hardly ate a bite. It wasn't that they didn't have an appetite, they were fasting and praying. Fasting is when you skip meals and use that time to pray, showing God that you are really serious.

Finally, two weeks passed, and Mom and Dad went to the doctor over in Charlotte. They watched as the doctor ran the ultrasound wand over Mom's belly, and Dad says that he immediately broke out into a great big grin. That spot on my brain had been burned into his mind; he knew exactly where it was, and exactly what it looked like. He also knew by looking at the ultrasound that it was gone!

The doctor looked at it hard, seeming utterly perplexed. He finally said, "Mr. and Mrs. Warner, I'm not sure what those technicians in your hometown saw, but there is absolutely nothing here; they must have been mistaken."

My Dad, still grinning, said, "No, Sir, they weren't mistaken; I saw it myself. But in the last two weeks we have been fasting and praying, and the Great Physician heard our prayers and healed our baby."

The doctor didn't seem to know what to say about that; he simply mumbled something congratulatory and left the room. So you see, I have every reason to trust Jesus. He has been taking care of me from the time I was in the womb, and I know He'll take care of me and my sisters now, even though I must admit, this "dream/not a dream" thing is surely a bit scary.

Chapter Three

As the train clickety-clacked on down the track, we were all lost in our own thoughts. We sat silently watching the mountains rush by and seeing cows on the hillsides and deer grazing in the occasional flat spot. The mountains here were nothing like those in North Carolina. There an occasional hill will seem to have popped up out of nowhere, destined to stand there lonely by itself. They had names like South Mountain, Kings Mountain, Crowders Mountain, mountains that were low and lonely in comparison to the mountains of West Virginia. Trying to think of a good way to describe that state, it finally dawned on me what it is like: West Virginia is like a giant piece of incredibly beautiful flat land, about the size of Texas that God smashed together from both ends making all the beauty go upward.

After about two hours, we felt the train beginning to slow. It continued to do so and gradually came to a stop in front of an old railroad depot. The conductor turned to us and said, "This is your stop, Children, you need to get off here."

Unsure of what else to do, we rose from our seats and started heading towards the door. But Carrie, always thinking ahead, turned back to the conductor and said, "Pardon me, but before we go, shouldn't you tell us what time to be back here so that you can pick us up and take us home? And shouldn't you also tell us whom we are looking for and what we are supposed to do when we find him?"

"I won't be picking you up," replied the conductor. "You will stay here till nightfall, go to sleep under the stars, and when you wake up in the morning, you will be back in your own beds. If you have not finished the job by then, I will pick you up again tomorrow night and bring you back here once again. As to whom you are looking for and what you are supposed to do when you find him, the answer to that question can be found in the little wooden church just down the way. And remember, you only have five days before it is too late." And with that, we found ourselves outside the train standing on an old wooden sidewalk with our transportation into this strange dream world chug-chugging away from us.

My dad always says that if a person has a choice between keeping his mouth open or his eyes open, he should always choose his eyes. We instinctively fell back on that lesson and stood firmly still for a few moments, surveying the surroundings. Ahead of us was the old wooden train depot, backed by steep hills covered with trees. The town, apparently called Callows, if the old wooden sign could be trusted, stretched away to the right.

The towns of the West Virginia coalfields sprang up haphazardly, hurriedly, beginning in 1883. I remembered from history class that that was the year the first shipment of coal was transported from these coal fields out to other areas by way of railroad. That started a population explosion, as good wages and inexpensive housing drew people from around the world.

Shanty towns went up seemingly overnight, and this was definitely one of them. A hundred feet or so to the right of the depot was a hotel/dining room/barber shop building. It was two short stories high, and we could hear music from an old tinny piano wafting its way through the cracks in the plank wood walls. The smell of beans and cornbread seemed to be riding on the music. My stomach started growling, but still we stood surveying the town.

Past the hotel was a livery stable, since most everyone in these mountain towns still owned and used horses. Past that was a jail that didn't look like it could hold a common shoplifter in if he really wanted to get out. Beyond that were two or three more buildings spread a little further out with signs like "Justice of the Peace," "Doctor Thompson, M.D.," and then came a big building, the nicest of all, with a large sign that said "Leeborough Mine Company Store." That building alone seemed to be impressive by the standards of the town.

After the company store, there was a hundred yards or so of an uphill climb and a tiny church sitting up on top of the hill. All of our eyes settled on that building, then after a moment we turned as one and looked at each other. "No use wasting time," Carrie said. "The conductor told us we would find our answers in the church."

"Like Dad always says," Aly began to reply, and we all said it with her, "More walk, less talk!" And our six feet started walking our three bodies toward one little church on the top of the hill in the midst of the valley.

Chapter Four

Soft sobbing. We all heard it at about the same time as we walked in the back of the church. It took a moment for our eyes to adjust to the minimal light drifting in through the stained-glass windows. Little by little we were able to see what was inside. The pews were wooden with no padding and though the furnishings were utterly simple everything was very clean. That was no small feat given the constant dust of a coal mining town. Up ahead of us was the simple altar stretching across the front of the low platform. Off to the left side of that altar we found the source of the crying. There was a lady, maybe in her thirties, kneeling by the altar pouring out the sorrow of her heart. She was unaware of our presence, and we felt positively bashful even being in there with her during such an obviously painful time for her. Finally, her crying subsided. She got very still, almost as if she was hearing a voice whispering in her ear–or maybe her heart. Dad always tells us that when we are praying we shouldn't do all the talking. Sometimes if we will just get quiet for a bit, the Lord Himself will speak back to us. Not into our ears or anything, but into our hearts which is sometimes just about as plain.

"Thank You, Lord, thank You," she said. "I don't know how, I don't know who, but thank You."

None of us knew what to do or say at that moment. The lady was still unaware of our presence, and the setting seemed so holy, so filled with the presence of the Lord, that we felt like trying to slip out without being noticed. But I have found that kind of thing is very hard to do, especially when your youngest sister has hay fever. Aly decided (well, she didn't really decide; I guess, it just sort of happened) to have a massive sneeze at that moment. One of those "I know I really shouldn't, but I can't help myself" kind of explosions that, now that I think of it, tends to happen in church more than any other place. That kind of thing tends to start a chain reaction, and sure enough it did. Aly sneezed. The woman screamed. Carrie and I jumped. My jump knocked over a small register stand that was beside me. Aly tried to catch it and in the process knocked my legs out from under me, sending me spiraling into Carrie, who ended up on top of me, with Aly on top of her, and the register stand underneath all of us. That hurt. We lay there groaning until soft hands started pulling us out of our jumbled mess. It was the lady at the altar, who had apparently composed herself enough to see that we three children were no threat and could in fact use her help.

"Whatever are you children doing in here, and where did you come from? You aren't from this valley; that much is obvious. There now, be careful. Just stand up and help me get all this sorted out. Good, good, no harm done."

When we were finally upright and untangled, I tried my best to begin the process of answering her questions, after thanking her profusely for getting us set straight and also apologizing for startling her.

"Ma'am, we are the Warner kids. I'm Kyle, this is Carrie, and this is Aly. You're right; we're not exactly from here. Our dad is a Baptist preacher, an evangelist, and we are in the area with him and Mom. He is preaching this week over in Boomer."

"Boomer?" She said, "Why, I know some good folks over in Boomer. But what brings you all the way out here, and where is your father now? And where exactly did you get those odd clothes?"

She said that, staring at us as if she had never seen carpenter jeans, Nike shoes, and dresses from Wal-Mart. It took a second for us to remember that she hadn't! Now, this could be a problem. How were we to explain our clothes to her, and even worse, how were we even to explain our presence there?

It's like this, Ma'am, we aren't actually

from here, and by "here" we mean the year 1912. In fact, we are from the future. 100 years in the future. Also, we are dreaming right now, but not really. A train conductor brought us here after we fell asleep and is coming back for us tonight.

Oh yeah, that would go over real well, I'm sure. Nothing like being locked up in an insane asylum 100 years before your time! We needed to think of something and fast. It was Carrie who, smooth as silk, dealt with the problem.

"We're here for a visit. Dad expects us to learn something everywhere we go (that was definitely true) and we are here to learn some things about coal, coal mining, life in mining towns, and the like. Our clothes are from the big city, you'll probably see some like them around here before you know it."

Her explanation seemed to satisfy the lady, so Carrie pushed on ahead.

"If you don't mind me asking, Ma'am, what were you praying and crying about? We didn't mean to intrude, but maybe the Lord brought us here for a reason. Is there anything we can do to help?"

I looked into the lady's very pretty but sad blue eyes. I could see tears welling up in them, like a cup under a faucet about to overflow. A tear escaped from both eyes almost at the same time and left little streaks down each side of her rosy face.

"I appreciate your kindness, but I don't think you will be able to help. This is going to take some serious help from the Lord."

"Ma'am," I said, "did I not just overhear you praying and saying that you didn't know who or how? Maybe we are the who and the how. I know we are young but so was David when he fought Goliath, so was the little lad whose lunch fed 5000, and so was Samuel when he started serving the Lord in the temple. Why don't you tell us what is going on, and who knows, maybe we can help after all."

For a moment, there was a profound silence, as no one said a word. The lady seemed to be thinking–evaluating what I had said. Then her shoulders slumped just a little, her head bowed a touch, and with seeming resignation she began to unfold her story.

"My son is missing. He is eleven years old, and I haven't seen him in two days. He went to work in the coal mine after my husband died last year. I think something bad has happened to him, but no one will tell me anything."

Carrie, Aly, and I stood there stunned. Eleven? What was an eleven-year-old boy doing working in a coal mine?

Seeming to sense our thoughts, maybe they were written on our faces, she continued: "Kids go to work in the coal mine younger than city folk may imagine. Especially when there is no dad in the home, boys will go to work and support the family. I didn't want him to go. I told him we would find another way, but Jonathan knew there really was no other way. So when I got up one morning several months ago, I found his bed empty and a note saying that he was going to work in the mine and would be back in the evening. He came back that night exhausted and filthy; the work was just way too hard and too heavy for him. But the next morning he was gone again and then back again the next night. He's been doing it for months now, up until two days ago, when he didn't come home. I went to the mine and spoke to the foreman and told him my son didn't come home from the mine."

"What did he say?" asked Aly.

"He told me to go home and mind my own business and that my boy was probably off playing in the hills somewhere. I've been back to the mine twice since then, and I'm still getting the same answer. Something has happened to my son, and no one at the mine will help me! My son is as responsible as a thirty year old. If he isn't home it isn't because he's off playing, it's because something has happened."

"Why don't you go in looking for him?" I asked.

"I tried this morning, but they blocked my way and wouldn't let me in. They said it was too dangerous. They left guards there to keep me out and just walked off into the mine carrying their tools. I didn't know what else to do, so I came here to pray."

"And that's when we showed up," I said. "That isn't a coincidence, Ma'am. My mom says there are no coincidences with God. We're obviously here for a reason, and this has got to be it. Ma'am, we are going to find your son."

Chapter Five

Outside on the street again Aly looked up at me and said, "Seriously? That was kind of a tall promise to make, don't you think? How exactly do you intend to keep it? What's your plan?"

Plan? Now that was a problem. I guess I didn't exactly have a plan now that she mentioned it.

"You don't have a plan, do you?" Carrie asked in a mock-surprise kind of voice. Then it was on to her own special "heavy with drama" kind of voice:

"Waaaaay to go big brother! Promise a crying mom we're going to find her son, lost somewhere in a coal mine and do so without a plan! Names come to mind at this point. Not names like MacArthur or Pershing or Roosevelt, mind you, more like Goofy and Donald and Daffy."

"Put a sock in it, Sis," I said. "The Bible says 'I can do all things through Christ which strengtheneth me.' " Yes, I know, falling back on a Bible verse at that moment was more of an escape mechanism for me than an actual act of faith, but it did get them to quit their yapping and that counted for something at least. Now I just needed to come up with a plan. Fast. It occurred to me that in order to find someone who had last been seen in a coal mine, one would need to look in the coal mine. But the problems with that were fairly large. One, we knew nothing about what things were like in a coal mine, and two, even if we did, the men running the mine would not be likely to let us outsiders in.

"Sis," I said to both Carrie and Aly, "we have some work to do." Quickly, I explained the two problems that we were facing. Then I said, "We can't get this done today. We are going to need to do some research on coal mines, and we can't exactly do that here and now. That will have to be done in our day when we won't be suspected of anything. But what we can do now is make some preparations. One of us has to go in that mine, and I am the only one who can. The men running the mine would never let you girls near it, but they won't let me near it either unless I look the part. Carpenter jeans and a church t-shirt will never do. I am going to have to come up with some clothes that will help me to fit in. Help me figure out where to buy clothes here in 1912."

28

"I think I can answer that," said Aly. "That Company Store we passed had clothes in the window that should be just right."

"Excellent, let's go!" and with that, we made our way to the Company Store and walked ourselves right inside.

Once we were inside the Company Store we set about acclimating ourselves to the surroundings. It was definitely not Wal-Mart. On the back wall were picks, hammers, shovels, and other metal tools that I could not identify. To the left was the counter with a clerk behind it eyeing us from under droopy eyelids, seemingly unconcerned about the three odd kids walking through his store. On a table near the front were hats with odd lamps mounted on top of them, and they were sitting beside cages with cute little canaries, chirping and flitting about. On the racks in the middle of the store were clothes, mining clothes, work pants and shirts that should fit the bill. In a matter of minutes we had gathered what I would need and realized we could afford them easily! The twenty-dollar bill I was carrying would go a long way in 1912; all of the clothes and tools I bought together came to only $4.75 cents.

Then it hit me…how was I going to pay for clothes in 1912 with a twenty-dollar bill from 2012? Talk about a way to attract unwanted attention. I stood there in fear, trying desperately to figure a way out of this mess. The clerk was staring at me with a *Are you going to pay or what?* kind of look on his face.

Aly stood beside me jerking on my arm, trying to get my attention. Finally, she stepped hard on my foot, and I snapped to attention. I looked at her, and she pointed to a sign on the counter. Well now, that sign just made matters even worse! For there on the counter, plain as day was a sign that said:

> **Company Scrip Only!**
>
> **No other currency accepted**

Seconds later the clothes were all back on the rack, and we were back outside on the street. None of us were saying anything but in just a moment Carrie started giggling and singing in a mock male bass voice:

> *"You load sixteen tons and what do you get? Another day older and deeper in debt. Now Gabriel don't you call me cause I can't go, I owe my soul to the company store."*

"Don't you remember Dad singing that?" she asked. "It's an old song about miners and mining companies. Even though the wages were good, the mining company would only pay the miners in company scrip, not real money. That way they had to shop in the company store. But since they had to shop there, the stores could charge whatever prices they want, no matter how high. That way, even if a man did get a raise or something, they could just charge him more for stuff and get their money right back. Men ended up having to get stuff from the company store on credit, and they never could work their way out of debt."

"Well that's just great," I said. "How am I going to earn the company scrip to buy the company clothes that will allow me access into the company mine, when I can't get into the mine without the company scrip to buy the company tools and clothes?"

"I think I know the answer to that," said Carrie. "Where do you get all kinds of old stuff, without anybody being suspicious?" The answer was clear immediately: we needed to find an antique store, a store in 2012, and get company scrip to bring back to the year 1912.

With nothing left that we could do for now in this odd, dream year of 1912, we headed a little ways off into the woods and waited for sundown. Remembering the conductor's last words to us, we knew that we would have to go to sleep under the stars and hope we woke up in our own beds back in the prophet's chamber of the Boomer Baptist Church. We settled down back in the trees and talked softly about our unsought for adventure while we watched the sun pull himself slowly towards the ground behind the hills overlooking the valley.

Chapter Six

The first thing that I remember was the droning of the air conditioner and the impression that I was cold. The room was very dark and my covers had slid off of me onto the floor sometime during the night. I tended to sleep "actively," which is another way to say I toss and turn a lot. I grabbed the edge of my blanket, pulled it up onto the bed again, and then sat straight up in bed like I had heard a gunshot! I remembered everything! I needed to... I needed to slow down and take a breath is what I needed to do. Whoa, what a dream! That was so incredibly real: the colors, the sounds, the smells. Wait till I tell Carrie and Aly about this!

"So what do we do now?" said Aly, who was apparently awake as well. "Should we tell Mom and Dad?"

Oh man, that sinking feeling in my gut was like a huge drop on a roller coaster in an

amusement park. Did it all really happen?
What about Carrie, did she have the same
dream/vision/thing as Aly and I?

"I don't think we can," I heard Carrie's
sleepy voice say. "They will think we are
absolutely nuts. Besides, what could they do
anyway? They weren't in the dream with us,
which means we are on our own in this. If we
tell them all they will do is worry."

"You're probably right," I said, "but we
are going to need their help, whether we tell
them what is going on or not. We need to get
them to take us somewhere to learn about coal
mines, and we need to get to an antique shop to
get some company scrip. So if they ask us what
we want to do today, we need to get them going
in that direction."

Moments later we were brushing teeth,
combing hair, ironing clothes and getting
dressed, then rushing out into the fellowship hall
for breakfast. Mom and Dad were there, as was
Pastor Neeson and his wife and kids. A nice
lady from the church was there as well, one of
those church secretaries that also cooks, cleans,
and generally does everything in the world that
needs doing. She and the pastor's wife had
prepared a delicious breakfast of pancakes,
eggs, and grits. We three kids ate like wolves,
hungry from all the activity we got while
sleeping last night. How odd is that?

Mom and Dad were talking to the pastor,
and he was asking them what they would like to
do today. They batted several possibilities

around but then our ears perked up when we heard Dad say, "Is there a coal mine we could tour? We like to learn something wherever we go, and I know the kids would love that."

Pastor Neeson proclaimed that he had just the thing. He told us that in Beckley there was an exhibition coal mine. We could tour it, taking a rail cart underground for a quarter of a mile and have a guide tell us what it was like in the mine back in the day.

How good is God! That is exactly what we needed. And so, two hours later, after several stops to get us to not be green around the gills, we drove into the parking lot of the exhibition coal mine in Beckley, West Virginia. Half an hour later we boarded an old railroad cart that had been converted to run on electric power and went underground into the dark of the mine.

Fortunately, the tour guide turned on the lights (after letting us sweat for a minute) and began to tell us about the mine.

"This was a working coal mine for twenty years, from 1890 to 1910. It goes five to six miles deep into the mountain. I worked in other mines for 26 years, and when I retired they let me sign on as a guide here part time. Once you go underground, it sort of gets in your blood, and it's hard to stay out."

It was clear that our guide enjoyed his new job. He stopped us at four points along the way. He pointed out the tools used in the olden days of mining: pick, shovel, breast auger, lights. The lights started out as little oil lamps hooked onto the miner's hat, but they would only last for an hour or so. So somewhere along the line, they developed carbide lights. It was a tin container of carbide. Screw another container of water onto it, strike it, and the combination produces a two or three inch flame that will last for three or four hours.

He shut off all the lights and spoke of that lamp. He said, "Miners made sure to become very familiar with their light. The last thing they wanted was to be alone in the mine, have their light go out, and be unfamiliar with it and not know how to get it refilled and relit."

In cases of dire need, boys started working in the mines as young as ten or eleven. We three kids looked at each other hard when he said that. Everyone was expected to pick and load at least six tons of coal per day. Good miners could do ten tons. The wage for doing so? 20¢ per ton! And if too much rock was in the cart, nothing at all. They would wear numbers down in the mine on pieces of metal and hang them on the side of the carts they filled. But often, other miners would take that number off and replace it with their own. So they got to where they would tack it to a piece of wood, put it in the bottom of the cart and then fill the cart up. When the cart was taken out and dumped, voila, there was their number.

They would work on their hands, knees, and bellies in a three-foot high space picking out the coal. Then when they had an area cleared, they would drill and blast the rest of it down since it now had a place to fall.

To shore up the roof they began by using timbers. Later they changed and used metal rods four feet long drilled up into the roof, securing the layers of rock together by making a beam out of the rocks. A rod went every four feet in every direction. In the 1970s they improved that yet again, utilizing a rod they would coat in epoxy, thus securing all the layers together and making them water-tight. That is still the system in use today.

Mines were graphed and laid out carefully, never going more than a few feet wide in any direction, thus leaving columns of coal to hold up the mountain. A few years ago in Utah, using a dangerous method called retreat mining, they took out a bunch of those columns, and the entire mountain collapsed and killed several men.

A danger in the mine was methane gas, so a man called the Fire Boss was in charge of burning pockets of it off. Another danger was Black Damp, which is an absence of oxygen. The timbers and the coal absorbed oxygen leaving none for the miners to breathe. Canaries were carried in little cages down into the mines, being very susceptible to that. If your canary keeled over, you knew you had to get out in a hurry. Oh, so that explained the cages in the general store with the cute little canaries! Carrie and I both looked over at Aly at the same time, and sure enough, she had that angry look on her face like she wanted to gnaw off the tour guide's leg with her teeth.

"Easy, Sis," I said. "It isn't his doing; he's just telling us the history that we need to know. But it does mean that I'll need a few more mining scrip dollars and my own canary." Well, that just made her start fuming at me! Girls–who can ever understand them?

A little while later we were back out into the sunlight touring the town that had been historically rebuilt around the mine. There was a village church, a miner's shanty, a miner's house, and the superintendent's house. That was nicer than anything I will likely ever have. All in all, an excellent experience. It ended right where we needed it to–in the gift shop.

There in the cases before us was mining scrip from various company stores. The nice lady behind the counter asked us if she could help us with anything, and I said, "Yes, Ma'am, do you have mining scrip from the Leeborough mine?"

I guess maybe that kind of a specific request is not one they get everyday. She just stopped, surprised, and when I looked over at my dad and Pastor Neeson, they were standing there with their jaws dropped as well.

"That's an awfully specific request, Son," said my dad. "How do you even know about any specific mines other than this one?"

That sort of put me on the spot. I didn't want to blab something true that would sound like a lie, but I didn't want to lie either! So I told the truth in a way that would get me off the hook–I hoped. "I guess I just dreamed it," I said then laughed a goofy laugh.

Dad just shook his head, and I heard him mumble quietly to Mom, "Are you sure that kid is actually ours?"

It took most all of the spending money we three kids had together, but we bought $15.00 worth of mining scrip from the Leeborough mine.

We left there and had lunch at a nearby pizza place, which was, all in all, an excellent experience. From there we went to a place called Bobby's Bargains and got some good books and other stuff very cheap.

We finally got back to church, Mom and Dad started working on their computers, and eventually, we had supper and then the night service. After church we went with the pastor's family to an ice cream shop for fellowship. Normally that would be all we had on our minds! After all, Rocky Road covered in caramel is hard to ignore. But as we sat in our seats, hearing the talk of all the adults around us, laughing, crying, joking, chit-chatting, it all sort of faded to a droning in my mind. I looked over at Carrie and Aly, and I could see that they felt the same way. What would happen when we got back to our beds in just a little while? Would last night prove to be just a weird, one-time "we must have been crazy" kind of thing, or would we board that train yet again?

Chapter Seven

Going to sleep that night was no easy job. How do you fall asleep when you are expecting to be awakened as soon as you do? I lay there, jingling the company scrip in my right pocket. It occurred to me that I had no idea if that particular idea would work. You can't take anything with you when you die, so could you take it with you when you dream? If not, we definitely had a problem.

It's funny how when you are thinking of falling asleep you can't, but as soon as you start thinking of anything else, like money in your pocket, you suddenly end up asleep without knowing it!

"Warner Children, come quickly!" came the voice from the conductor.

In a flash we were sitting up straight at the exact same old train depot as the night before. I reached for my right pocket and breathed a sigh of relief as we all stood up.

Apparently you could take things with you into a dream/not a dream–at least in this one. Quickly we boarded the train, and a moment later we were clickety-clacking back down the track through the same valleys and by the same mountains as the night/day before.

When we arrived back in Callows, the conductor turned to us and said, "You did well on your first day. But remember that you have only four more days, after which it will be too late for him."

We stepped off the train again, and a moment later it was clickety-clacking and chuggity-chugging away from us yet again, leaving us in the strange dream world to find a little boy lost in the mines. Without a word we made our way back to the company store. We gathered the same supplies we had gathered yesterday (along with the canary) while the same droopy-eyed clerk watched us with seeming indifference. The dusty counter was barely big enough to fit everything as we laid it in front of the clerk. Lazily, he removed his pencil from behind his ear, which my mom would have demanded that he wash immediately, (the ear, not the pencil) licked it (the pencil, not the ear), and added it all up on a piece of paper.

"That'll be $6.25, in Leeborough mining scrip." He said that last line as if he expected me not to have it. But when I pulled the money from my pocket and placed it on the counter in front of him, he just shrugged, handed me my change, bagged everything up, and told us to have a nice day.

The door clanged shut behind us, and we were back out on the street. We didn't know where to go from there. We didn't exactly have a home here in 1912 for me to get dressed in. We looked at each other, and without a word, we knew exactly where to go. When in doubt, church is always the answer for us! We walked up the hill, into the church, and sure enough, the same sweet mother was at the altar praying yet again. She must have heard us this time when we came in, for she practically leaped up from the altar to meet us.

"You came back! I wasn't sure if you would," she said.

"Ma'am," Carrie answered, "we Warners keep our word. My brother promised you we would find your boy, and we intend to keep that promise."

Quickly we explained to her our plan, for me to go into the mine as a worker and look for her Jonathan. She looked a bit worried at that and told us that it would not work.

"The mine boss isn't hiring anybody right now, what with the coal war brewing. Company men are everywhere and no hiring is allowed," she said.

"That's not a problem," I said. "I'm not working for a paycheck; I'm working to find your son. No one is going to question me walking into the mine with all of the other workers as if I am already an employee. I don't need them to give me a number, since I'm not trying to earn any money. Any work I do, any carts I fill, I can just send out without a number. Someone else will no doubt take credit for it, so no one will suspect anything."

That seemed to quiet her doubts. All we needed now was to settle on Carrie and Aly's part in all of this. They obviously could not come into the mines, but they sure as shootin' weren't going to sit around and do nothing; they had too much Warner in them for that.

'Little Sis and Littler Sis," I said, "here's what I need from you. I need you to use your ears and get me as much information as you can out here while I am in there. Ma'am, where do the other miner's kids hang out at during the day?"

It took me a minute to realize why she was just staring at me blankly. "Hang out" was definitely not a 1912 kind of term!

"I'm sorry, there I go talking in my big-city words again," I said, "where could my sisters go to play or fellowship with the other miners' children?"

Her face immediately lit up with recognition at that, and she said, "Why, most of them will be with their mothers working at home, doing dishes, cooking, and other chores. But it just so happens that there is a quilting festival going on this week here in Callows. That means that in the early afternoons the ladies and young kids will meet by the creek, have a pot-luck lunch, and then the moms and older girls will quilt while the younger kids play."

"That's exactly what we need," I said. "Carrie, Aly, go with..." and then it dawned on me that I didn't even know this sweet lady's name! "Ma'am, I'm sorry, what is your name?"

"My name is Sarah, Sarah Templeton. You may call me Mrs. Sarah."

"Mrs. Sarah," I said, "Would you please do me a favor? While I am in the mine looking for your son, would you please watch after my sisters? They are very smart and able to handle themselves, but since we aren't from around here, I'd feel better if I knew an adult was keeping eyes on them."

Carrie and Aly glared at me with that *we can take care of ourselves* kind of look, but Mrs. Sarah said, "Why, of course, I will."

"Sis and Sis, go with Mrs. Sarah to that quilting festival. Play games, introduce yourselves to the other kids. Listen carefully. Try and find out something, anything that the kids may have overheard from their parents. Somebody knows something and that somebody may have accidentally let their kids overhear it."

Moments later, after having changed clothes and stowed my "our time" clothes in our nightly meeting place, I was walking away from them heading for the entrance to the mine with the sun rising over the mountains and warming my muscles, which I figured were in for some serious soreness by day's end.

Chapter Eight

When you fall in with a group of weary looking men and boys and trudge wearily along with them, it is surprisingly easy to walk right into a coal mine. After all, who in their right mind would be going into the mine unless they were actually an employee? No employee number, no paycheck. But I wasn't going into the mine for a paycheck, I was going into the mine to find a missing eleven-year-old boy whose mother was praying for his safe return. I knew that he had to still be alive, because according to the conductor we still had four more days to help him.

It is hard to describe the experience of going into a coal mine in the year 1912 to anyone in our time. We are so used to good ventilation, pleasant working conditions, and safety regulations. Going into that coal mine was a shock to the senses all the way around. For starters, even a few feet into the mine wasn't really well lit. I expected it to be lit somehow all the way to the point at which we were to be digging, more than a mile back into the mountain. But within 15 to 20 feet, my eyes were having to adjust to very dim conditions, with only minimal lighting. And then there was the air itself. The ventilation was terribly poor; as athletic as I am, I was laboring to breathe and hadn't even swung the first pick yet. I lit my lamp while walking, and the little two-inch flame sprung to life and lit the pathway in front of me just a bit better.

It took about 15 minutes to get to the spot where we would be working. I was a little nervous, no, a lot really, hoping that I would not immediately stand out as someone who had no clue what he was doing. If I did, I figured this rescue attempt would be very short-lived.

A kid in my church is fond of saying, "When you don't know what to do, stall!" I fell into that advice, spending a minute or so fiddling with my suspender straps, adjusting, adjusting, re-adjusting. All the while, out of the corner of my eye, I was watching a man who appeared to have been in the mine for many years as he began his work. Within that minute of stalling, I had a pretty good idea of what to do. I went to a spot twenty feet or so further into the mine, grabbed a very short-handled pick, and started hacking away at a point on the side about three feet above the ground. I noticed that the coal was being cut out at the three-foot level and then the miners would slide on their backs into the crease they were cutting and continue to hack away with that short-handled pick. I was a bit surprised, having expected the mining to be done head-high or better. But since everyone else was working lying on their backs, I was soon on mine.

Hard work is one thing. Mining, I quickly learned, goes beyond simply being "hard work." Within a half an hour or so, my shoulders, back, and arms were all screaming. My hands were blistering right through the gloves. My lungs felt like they were about to explode. But my dad taught me not to be a quitter, ever, so I kept swinging the pick, with a steady "Thunk! Thunk! Thunk! Thwap!"

The "thwap" brought everything to a halt–literally. My swing had only gone about half-way and then stopped in midair! I looked up and back and saw a large, gloved hand holding my pick by the handle. That large hand was attached to a massive, muscled-up arm. My eyes followed that arm up to the shoulder, then from the shoulder onto the face. I was staring backwards at a really powerful looking man with some of the kindest eyes I had ever seen.

"Son," he said, "stop for a minute and take a rest. It's real clear that you aren't used to this, but I'm impressed with your work ethic. Take a breather for a couple of minutes and let me show you a thing or two."

With that, I gratefully slid to a seated position against the wall, while the man I immediately nicknamed "The Miner from

Heaven" took my pick and showed me exactly how to do the job. His skill was clear, and I saw quickly that muscles in the arms were not all that was needed in this job. This man had a mind as strong as his arms, and that made a huge difference in the work. He showed me what to look for, where to strike with the pick, the best way to use the flat shovel to remove the coal and put it in the cart, and how to brace up the undercut as I went. The fifteen minutes he spent helping me was worth a month of school as far as I was concerned.

When he finished teaching and handed me back my pick, I said, "Thank you Sir, so very much!"

He smiled down at me and said, "Jackson, my name is Jackson, and you are welcome." But the next words he said chilled me all the way to the bone, "Now, seeing as how you and I both know you don't have an employee number, why don't you tell me what you are doing down here in this mine?"

Chapter Nine

My heart raced, and my hopes sunk. I didn't want to lie, but I knew that "the truth, the whole truth, and nothing but the truth" would land me in an insane asylum, a jail, or worse. I stood there shaking, wondering what to do, looking at the face of the big man called Jackson–which seemed to have gone completely cold and stern. My eyes went to the floor and stayed. Awkward seconds of silence passed between us and then the silence was finally broken... by low laughter. I looked up and the smile was back on Jackson's face. My eyes searched his to see if I could discern what he was thinking, but he spoke and cleared that part up for me.

"Young man, you have a good baritone singing voice. I like that. It's a good thing you use it for the Lord, otherwise I might be tempted to think you are up to no good."

I had been singing! While Jackson picked away and I sat, I had been doing as I often do and absentmindedly been singing one of our church hymns–an old one, "Brethren we have met to worship." It occurred to me that Jackson, in between strokes of the pick, had joined me once or twice.

"I sing in the little church on the hill," he said. "Good Lord gave me a voice; I figure I best use it for Him. I got saved as a boy, and you are obviously one of that number yourself. Now, since you know we are family, why don't you let me know why you're down here? You are obviously all alone, at least down here in this mine, and that can be a dangerous thing. You need somebody to trust, and the Lord is speaking to my heart telling me to be that person. So before the mine boss comes by and sees us talking on company time, spill the beans. Why are you here?"

If I was ever going to take a chance, I felt like this would be a good time to do it. God seemed to have brought the big man right into my pathway when I needed him. So I lowered my voice, moved in a step closer to him, and began to speak in a near whisper.

"Brother Jackson, you got me. I am not supposed to be here in this mine (I left out the part about 1912). But there is a crying mama named Sarah that my sisters and I met in the little church on the hill. She says that her eleven-year-old son has been working in the mine and didn't come home a couple of nights ago and hasn't been heard from since."

"Mrs. Sarah," he said. "That name doesn't rightly ring a bell. But then again, there's a heap of people in that little building of a Sunday, and I only know a few of them. But a boy lost in the mine, that can't be a good thing. Why doesn't she go to the mine boss or the foreman and have him set up a search of the mine?"

"She did," I said "and she was told to go home and not to worry about it. The next couple of days she went back, some men blocked her way and won't let her in and won't give her any information. She is sure they are hiding something."

"And so you have come into the mine to try and find him? Without ever having been in a mine before? Not knowing the first thing about what you are doing? That was your plan?"

Hearing him put it that way reminded me a lot of my sister, but I wasn't about to tell him that. It turns out I didn't have to, because he positively belly-laughed at me under his breath just a second later.

"Boy," he said, "that's the dumbest but bravest thing I've ever heard of. I'm proud of you. But I can tell you this, you have no idea what you are getting into. Get back to work, and we'll talk about it a bit at lunchtime."

The next few hours were filled with more picking, more laying on my back, and much more shoveling. The lessons Jackson gave me paid off well, I actually got two carts filled and sent out by lunchtime. *That ought to make some dishonest person very happy*, I thought to myself as I sent the carts without ID numbers out of the mine to be weighed and counted.

There is no way to tell by sight when lunchtime is down in a coal mine, since the mine never sees the sunshine. But the miners seemed to have an internal clock for that sort of thing. Almost at once, the sound of picks and shovels died away in the mine and were replaced by the sound of shuffling feet, men sitting down by the wall, and metal lunch pails being opened. I followed their lead and sat down to eat the lunch Mrs. Sarah had provided for me.

A few minutes into devouring my sandwich, Jackson sat down beside me and in just a few bites devoured his own lunch. He seemed to be in a hurry to do so, clearly wanting to have some time to speak with me.

"So," he began, "if you are going to find a little boy either lost or killed or for some reason held in a coal mine, you might need to know a bit about what is going on in the world of West Virginia coal, because everything usually ties together somehow. How familiar are you with the coal war?"

"I've heard of it," I answered truthfully as I thought back to our first night with the train conductor, "but I have no real idea what is going on concerning it. What can you tell me?"

"Plenty," he said. "Coal is all about money, just like most everything else. And like the Good Book says, 'the love of money is the root of all evil.' In this case, the root takes the form of dishonesty by the mine bosses. Each and every cart sent out of here is weighed, and the miners are paid by the weight. But the carts, which are supposed to hold roughly 2,000 pounds, have seemed to get suspiciously just a tad bit bigger these last few months. But the scales show that they are still holding the same 2,000 pounds. Furthermore, the mine bosses do all of the weighing: no miners are allowed to be there to watch it.

"Then there is the fact," he continued, "that rock isn't paid for. For every piece of rock a miner's pay is lessened. But once again, no miners are allowed to be there to see that process; we just have to take the bosses' word for it. A few months ago some of the miners began demanding fairer treatment, including having a representative of the miners be there during the weighing process."

"That sounds reasonable," I said. "How did they respond?"

"How greedy men always respond," he answered, "by threatening the miners. They have brought in security men. They wave their guns around; they threaten to do harm to the miners or their families; things are getting very tense. There has been talk of the miners banding together to fight back, but that kind of talk has led to threats from the governor to send in troops against us. If something doesn't change, a lot of blood is going to be shed."

"Wow," I said, "That sounds like a whole lot of trouble. But I can't see any way that all of that could tie in with a missing little boy. Any ideas?"

"Nope," he said, "none at all. But I do know that evil men are never just evil in one way or in one area. If men will stoop to stealing, cheating, and threats of violence, it isn't hard to see that they would also be capable of harming a little boy for some reason."

I considered that and had to agree that he was right. But that still brought me no closer to finding that little boy, and a second day/night was rapidly getting away from me. I leaned over to Jackson once more and said, "I need a way to search the mine without anyone knowing about it."

"That shouldn't be too hard," he said. "Just crawl way back up under a ledge a few minutes before quitting time and wait until everyone leaves. There will be men guarding the entrance to make sure no one gets in after hours, but no one would ever think of somebody not coming out at quitting time."

I considered that and realized that while it might work, it did present a couple of other problems. One, I would also have to find a way to get back out to get to Carrie and Aly. I had no idea what would happen if we weren't together to go to sleep under the stars like the conductor told us. Would they wake up at home without me? That would be hard to explain. The second problem was that when I didn't come out on time and meet up with them, they would absolutely freak out. My sisters' freaking out is not a good thing. Carrie would be at the mine in under a minute trying to gnaw off the guard's leg like a rabid beaver. Aly would be right behind her doing the head wagging, hip shaking, finger pointing, "You tell me where my brother is right now, or I'm a fittin' to open a can of whoop down and pour it all over you!"

Quickly, I wrote out a note explaining my plan to Carrie and Aly. I handed it to Jackson and said, "I need a favor. When you leave here tonight, please go by the creek to where the quilting festival is being held. Look for a lady with two girls. The older girl will have long black hair, the younger one shoulder length blonde hair. To make sure you have found the right ones, ask them if they can do the Shimei Shake. If they say 'yes,' give them the note."

Jackson stood there looking perplexed for just a moment. Finally he said, "The Shimei Shake?"

"The Shimei Shake," I repeated. "It's a message my dad preached once about Shimei from the Bible. He is the only preacher I know unusual enough to preach a message like that. It is Carrie's favorite; she will know immediately that you have been talking to me."

"The Shimei Shake, huh? I'd like to hear your dad preach sometime," he said as he turned to go back to his work.

I thought to myself *all you need to do is live another hundred years or so,* and I went back to work myself. The coal wasn't going to pick and shovel itself into a cart, so I figured I better get at it hard for the next several hours.

Chapter Ten

Hi, this is Carrie. I'll pick up the story for this chapter since Kyle was down in the mine and had no way of knowing what was going on up top. Aly and I had gone that day to the quilting festival down by the creek, just like we all planned. It was a good thing our mom had taken us to Alabama from time to time to hang out with grandmas and great-grandmas, because we had learned a thing or two about quilting from them. We quickly fell in with others around us, little girls, young women, new brides, middle-aged mothers, and matronly grandmothers. The very little children played and romped and hooted and hollered, and all in all it was a noisy, happy kind of event.

But Aly and I were there for information. We quilted and chatted and walked about from time to time, and in general, eavesdropped on everyone we possibly could. Eavesdropping was normally wrong, I guess, but wouldn't it be ok in a situation like this? I sure hoped so, I didn't need any more sin to repent of. I still wasn't sure I had been forgiven for putting itching powder in Kyle's sleeping bag last month! I really got blistered for that one, but as much as I hate to admit it, it was worth it, and I hope I get a chance to do it again.

Anyway, we meandered and socialized and eavesdropped, and over all, we got nothing. I was getting frustrated and just a little bit desperate when I happened to wander by a rather haughty looking young woman, who was also a bit of a loud mouth. She reminded me of the woman spoken of in Proverbs 7:11, which says "She is loud and stubborn; her feet abide not in her house." I made up my mind right then and there to nickname her "Las," which stood for "Loud and Stubborn."

I went to the creek just behind Las, knelt down, and began to wash my arms and face slowly in the cool water. All the while, I was listening while Las was blabbering on to a couple of other haughty looking women.

"Well, I know I probably shouldn't say anything, but I know you girls will understand, not like the rest of this rabble," she said, while gesturing to pretty much everyone in the area that was not her or her two friends. "Everybody is worried about a war between the miners and the government," she continued in a far lower voice, almost a whisper, "but it might not be such a bad thing after all. The miners wouldn't stand any chance at all of winning, but since there would be bloodshed on both sides, the government would be forced to step in and take control over the mines. That means the present ownership would be, shall we say, 'removed from the equation.' And that would leave an opening in the ownership department for any men that had been shrewd enough to cut their deals with the authorities ahead of time."

I looked back over my shoulder and could see the side of Las's face as she said those last words. She seemed to me to have an evil, wicked grin on her face as she said it. I thought to myself *I bet that her man has already cut that deal and has probably been joined by whatever wimpy men those other two Jezebels are leading around by the nose.*

Something about that woman, her arrogance, her perceived superiority, really set me off. I probably shouldn't have, but I decided to lower her a peg or two while relieving her of certain bits of information that I needed.

"Pardon me, Ma'am," I said as I rose and sauntered innocently over to her. "Are you the wife of one of the miners? Because that dress seems awfully fine for a simple miner's wife. However do you two afford such things? Do you sell quilts to help him make enough money for the household?"

"I am most certainly NOT the wife of a miner, Girl," she said angrily. "Do I look like I would be married to a miner? Do you think there is a miner on or under this good earth that could ever win the hand of a woman like me?

61

How dare you! I am the wife of the mine boss himself, Cyril McBride."

"Oh, I'm so sorry, Mrs. McBride," I said, "I just thought that even if you didn't look like a miner's wife, you certainly sounded like one, what with all of the misplaced modifiers, dangling participles, and general grammatical flaws in your speech, along with clear enunciation problems that could probably be helped by extended speech therapy. My bad."

I turned quickly and walked away, putting my vocabularic sword back in its sheath and concealing a pleased grin. I knew I would be half way across the festival grounds before she was even able to process the fact that she had just been insulted. Like dad always says, "Only dumb people with a limited vocabulary need to cuss. If you develop a good vocabulary, you can positively insult a person as badly as they deserve it and leave them scratching their heads wondering what you just said."

The verbal lashing had not been my goal. My goal had been to gather information, and I was pretty sure I had just struck pay-dirt. I didn't know how it tied into our missing little boy, but the fact that the mine boss wanted a coal war to break out and had taken steps to ensure that he himself would end up on top of the smoking rubble that remained was not likely to be a coincidence.

I was just stepping back into the little circle with Aly and Mrs. Sarah when a shadow fell over all of us. I looked up and back and gasped a little. There was a man behind me, a big man, with arms maybe even as strong as my dad. I felt instantly like running, feeling like maybe Las hadn't been so dumb after all and had sent some thug after us.

But before I could decide on fight or flight, (Fight? What would I have done, gnawed at his leg like a rabid beaver?) the big man spoke: "Pardon me young ladies, but do you by chance know the Shimei Shake?"

He said those words as if he felt like the dumbest human in the world for asking such a thing, but Aly and I were laughing almost immediately. "We sure do," Aly said, "and the fact that you know about it tells me that you've been talking to our brother, Kyle."

The big man looked relieved and lowered his voice as he said, "I certainly have, Miss. He and I just so happen to be brothers, if you know what I mean. Are you our sisters?"

"Sure we are," I answered, "both of us. It's nice to meet another member of the family. So, brother, who are you?"

"My name is Jackson," he said with a low laugh. "I met your brother in the mine today, and he told me why he is in there."

At that, Sarah and Aly and I all three looked at each other, unsure if we should trust this big man. But he immediately reached into his pocket and pulled out a folded letter. "Your brother told me to give this to you." Quickly I opened it and read what Kyle had sent to us:

Carrie and Aly,

I haven't found Jonathan yet, but I have learned some things that may tie into his disappearance. The man I sent to you with this note is Jackson, he is a friend. I am staying in the mine after hours, and snooping around to see what I can find. I will stay exactly three hours, and then I will need to come out so we can 'get some sleep.'

I knew what he meant by that and so did Aly. I dropped my eyes back to the letter and began to read again.

When it comes time for

me to leave, I will need some help. There are guards by the mine keeping people out after hours, but they will also end up keeping me in! I need you to distract them, just long enough for me to get out, then we will meet up at the spot.'

Kyle

Great. It was just like my brother to need a distraction and not give us any clue how to accomplish that task. Fortunately, we were girls, which meant we had the intelligence to do the job.

Chapter Eleven

As Jackson left the mine to go take my message to Carrie and Aly, I snuffed out my head lamp and made a quick dive way back under a shelf of coal. I laid there very quiet and still for what had to be 45 minutes. I wanted to make ultra sure that everyone was out of the mine before I went snooping around. Finally, satisfied that everyone was gone, I re-lit my lamp.

A coal mine is scary enough when there are hundreds of miners in there along with you. When you are by yourself, it is downright spooky. But I couldn't let fear get in the way, not with a mother counting on me to find her little boy. So I crawled out from under the ledge, got my bearings, and went snooping.

I was amazed at just how big this mine was. It had to have been in operation for decades. It stretched out down multiple corridors and in three different directions: straight ahead, to the right, and to the left, going back up under the mountain for miles. If the Lord didn't help me, there was no way the time I had would be enough. So I fired up a quick prayer, picked a direction, the corridors to the right, and headed farther back into the mountain.

It is a very good thing for me that I have my mom's sense of direction rather than my dad's. Dad is perfect at almost everything, but when it comes to finding his way in or out of anywhere, he is, as he puts it, "directionally challenged." He and Mom were headed home from West Virginia after a meeting he preached before we were born, and they had a little problem. Mom was sleepy and needed to take a nap while he drove. So she told him, "Just stay on this road, I-77 South, and it will take you straight to Charlotte, and I know you can get us home from there." Then she went to sleep.

Dad, bless his heart, had this thing figured out. He was in his lane, that lane would take him to Charlotte, and the devil himself was not going to get him out of that lane. What he did not realize is, right about Wytheville, that lane ceased to be I-77 South and became I-81 North! An hour and a half later, Mom woke up, blinked a couple off times, looked at a sign, shot straight up in her seat and shouted, "Fincastle! What are we doing in Fincastle!"

Dad had gone 90 miles the wrong way and had to turn around and go 90 miles back just to get to where he went wrong. I guess that just goes to show two things: one, always follow the directions, which is a good analogy for living by the Bible, and two, never let Dad drive while Mom is asleep.

Anyway, I headed off into the mine to the right, hoping and praying I could find a missing little boy or at least find something to get me closer. The corridors were all about the same size, ten feet wide and about seven feet tall. Off of those main corridors would be smaller ones, only five or six feet wide, shooting sideways into the mountain, then looping back onto the next one, making a small city-block type of arrangement. I wandered down each main and side corridor in the direction I was going, for what must have been a mile or two. Every corridor was the exact same. The three feet shelves, once dug out and removed, had then been busted out at the seven foot level. That let me know what I would be doing in my own spot tomorrow if I had to come back.

After what seemed like forever, I hit the end of the series of corridors that I had been traveling and searching. It just came to an end, like a hallway in a house. I glanced at my watch, which I had kept hidden in my overall pockets, illuminated the dial and realized that I was running out of time. I had accomplished much without accomplishing anything. By that I mean that I had not found Jonathan, but I had at least eliminated everything to the right, roughly one-third of the mine.

I had fifteen minutes to get to the mine entrance, where I was counting on Carrie and

Aly providing me with the distraction I would need to get out. Dad and Mom and I were in the habit of running 5k races together, so I should be able to cover the distance in time with no problem. I started off on a fast run and was covering the ground in a hurry. It looked like I would arrive at the entrance of the mine early... until I felt my toe snag on what felt like a shovel left in the pathway! I went flying head over heels, tumbling and crashing into something; it felt sort of like a coal cart. I lay there groaning for just a minute, my eyes closed wincing in pain, then I opened my eyes and saw nothing. My light was out. No, feeling my head I knew it was even worse than that. It wasn't out, my light was gone!

Chapter Twelve

As I lay there panting in the pitch darkness, I could feel hot fear rising up in my throat. I put my hand an inch in front of my nose and could not see it at all, not even an outline. It was so incredibly dark that unless you have experienced it, it almost defies description. I remembered my dad often preaching about the outer darkness of the lake of fire and heard him tell how those who reject Jesus will burn and fall forever, yet never be able to see a thing, and I thought that this darkness must be something like that. As scared as I was, I could not help but feel sorry for anyone who dies without Jesus and goes to that awful place. I knew that even some of my family probably did not know him, and I felt a quick tear streak down my face as I uttered a quick prayer for them to be saved.

I didn't have much time though, I knew that, so once I said "amen," I got to my hands and knees and felt around trying to find my light. After several frantic moments, I realized that I was simply not going to find it. I reached for my watch to use its illuminated dial and found that it had been shattered in the fall. At a moment like that, a person really needs to control his emotions and think clearly. Proverbs 25:28 says, "He that hath no rule over his own spirit is like a city that is broken down, and without walls." It means that if you cannot control your emotions and reactions, you are defenseless. Thinking of that, I slowed my breathing down, cleared everything out of my mind, and asked the Lord for wisdom for what to do. I had to get to the entrance of the mine, fast, but I could not see! What could I use since I had no light and could not use my eyes?

Within a split second, the answer hit me: the mine corridors were utterly consistent. Same width, same length, same layout. If a person could figure out how many steps were in each one, he could count himself out of a mine. Quickly, I found the corner that started the next corridor. I took big steps, to account for the fact that I would be trying to run, and I counted twenty steps per corridor. If I could take those twenty steps with my left hand against the wall, I would be able to feel by the openings when I was crossing over the narrow corridors. When I got to one twice that size, I knew it would be the main corridor at which point I could turn left, keep my hand on the wall, and sprint towards the entrance.

All of this I knew in my head and in my heart, but I could not see any of it. It was just like the Biblical admonition that "we walk by faith and not by sight." I grinned at that, put my hand to the wall, and took off. Sure enough, the twenty step pattern held true followed by two steps as I crossed over a small corridor. That happened time after time after time, till I finally realized that two steps had become four! I slid to a stop, turned left, put my hand on the wall, and broke into an all-out sprint. I was running out of time; I just prayed that I could make it. If I didn't, the girls were going to be most unhappy with me.

After a lung-burning sprint, the air began to change, getting fresher and sweeter. That let me know that I was nearing the entrance of the mine. I slowed to a jog, trying to get my labored breathing under control. I didn't want to be gasping for air so loud that the mine guards heard me. After a few more steps I slowed to a walk. I could now see the light of the moon and the guard lights as well seeping into the mine. A few steps closer and I stopped entirely, lay down on my stomach, and began to crawl. Sixty seconds of that brought me to the edge of the mine. I looked over the lip of the ground... and saw two guards standing just a few feet in front of me. I was here. I had run in the dark to get here. Where, oh where, were my sisters and my distraction?

When it finally came, I had to clamp my hand over my mouth to keep from laughing right out loud. It was so simple, yet so brilliant. It would not have thrown anyone in 2012, but in 1912 a laser pointer was definitely going to get some attention! Aly always carried one around in her pocket, one of those $5.00 toy store models that teachers always confiscated on the very first day of school. I watched as a red dot appeared on the ground in front of those two men, just circling slowly right in front of them. I heard the first one, the guy on the right, gasp as he saw it. He quickly poked his buddy, who gasped himself. They stood there, transfixed, not sure what evil new sorcery this was or what to do about it. Aly was really playing this well!

Suddenly, the evil dot leaped from the ground and landed on the leg of the guy on the right. I have heard it said that white men can't dance. I can assure you that that is definitely not true! That guy cut a rug like he was trying to shake a demon off, but the evil dot just stayed with him, moving from his leg to his chest and back. Finally, Aly sent the red dot back to the ground in front of the two men. They stayed there, semi-crouched in front of it, not knowing what to do or how to fight this substanceless enemy.

And then Aly swung for the fences. The dot leaped up off of the ground and landed right on the forehead of the guy on the left. He could not see it there, but his buddy sure did!

Do you remember the Three Stooges? When guy on the right reached for the shovel beside him and swung for the fences at guy on the left's face, it looked like a scene from those old black-and-white movies. Left guy forgot about the evil dot and ducked the swinging shovel of his buddy, who was for some reason now trying to smash his face in. He dove into his buddy's mid-section, and the two of them went rolling head over heels over the edge of the hill, crashing into the woods below. I had thought I was going to have to sneak out of the mine like a CIA operative, but instead, I was able to walk out, laughing, to meet my two genius sisters. A few minutes later we were at our sleep spot, under the stars, waiting for our nightly trip home.

Chapter Thirteen

Once again we awakened to the droning of the air conditioner. None of us had to ask this time, we all knew that what was happening was real. I looked over at Aly and said, "Good call on the laser light. Whatever we are going to need tonight, make sure it's with you in bed." She just grinned that toothy grin that means *You got it, Bro!*

It is hard to get into the routine of showers, teeth brushing, and general hygiene when your mind is on an adventure like the one we were involved in. But the fact that my dad would paddle our tails if we didn't do those things was pretty good motivation. So a half hour later we were dressed and ready and out into the fellowship hall with Pastor Neeson and his family. It was waffles and syrup today, and not a one of us was going to complain about that.

As we sat eating our breakfast quietly, letting the adults talk like well-mannered children should, we heard Pastor Neeson ask my dad what he would like to do today.

After a bit of discussion, we loaded up in the church van and went to a place called Hawks Nest, a huge crest overlooking the river. Beside that winding river was a train of about 120 cars, winding and meandering its way along. Pastor Neeson said that it had about two million dollars of coal in it. I couldn't help but wonder if the grandsons or great-grandsons of big Jackson were the ones who had dug it out of the ground and loaded it onto those railway cars.

To the left, way down in the river basin, there was a set of huge gates that open to a tunnel under the mountain that allows the river to cascade through when it is needed for power production.

From there we went to Babcock state park and spent a few hours there. There is a picturesque grist mill there and a beautiful river. It is one of the most photographed spots in West Virginia. We had a picnic lunch there. We stopped in the gift shop, browsed a while, and then came on back to the church. The service went pretty well, but it was a bit of a lower crowd than last night. After service we went with the pastor's family down into Montgomery to the DQ, where Mom was able to get a wi-fi signal to pay some bills. We enjoyed the day, we enjoyed the service, we enjoyed the ice cream and fellowship afterward, but we three kids were anxious to get back to the prophet's chamber and get to sleep, so we could wake up and get back on the train to find the missing boy.

As I sat thinking about those things, I heard Carrie let out a low hissing noise through her teeth. Aly and I looked over at her, and she said in a low voice, "I forgot to tell you what I learned at the quilting festival!"

The three of us in unison looked over at the adults seated at other tables. Sure enough, they were engrossed in their own conversations and weren't paying much attention to us. I could hear my dad talking to the Pastor about some people whom our home church had helped a great deal through the years, who had recently turned right around and done a lot of harm to our pastor and church.

"I am seeing those kinds of things happening to churches around the country," Dad said, "People seem to have forgotten that they will reap what they sow."

Pastor Neeson nodded in agreement, and as he started speaking himself, the three of us turned to each other and lowered our heads near to each other where we could whisper.

"I met a woman today at the quilting festival. She was a snotty thing, but fortunately for us she also has a loud mouth. Her last name is McBride, and she is married to the mine boss. I overheard her talking about the possible coal war that the conductor warned us about. It seems that there are some people that actually want the war to break out, and her husband seems to be at the top of that list. She was saying that if the war between the miners and the government does break out, it would cause the government to remove the present owner of the mine. I think her husband has made some kind of a deal with them to become the new owner when that happens."

"Whew!" I said, "They would go from being average folks to being filthy rich overnight! That's some pretty serious incentive to do wrong. But what in the world could Jonathan have to do with this? He's a little boy, for goodness sakes."

"I don't know," Aly said between slurps of her chocolate milkshake, "but the two things have to tie together somehow."

As I looked at the chocolate ring forming around her lips, I considered that and quickly concluded that she was probably right. Somehow, some way, that little boy had managed to get himself mixed up in the middle of a world-class crime that was going to involve intentional bloodshed and the theft of a mine worth hundreds of millions of dollars even in 1912. We had to find that kid, fast, before he ended up squashed like a bug by people wearing some very big boots.

I knew it had to be getting pretty late, so I raised my left arm to look at my watch, and when I did, I couldn't help but feel like I had been kicked in the gut. I turned ashen white, and both Carrie and Aly noticed. I held my watch up for them to see, and the crystal over the display was shattered. I had gone an entire day without even looking at it. Now that I did, the ramifications of what I was seeing hit me like a ton of bricks.

"I broke this in the mine last night. It's still broken here in 2012. We haven't even thought to ask the question, but it appears we already have our answer. If something breaks while we are in this dream/not a dream, it seems that it will still be broken when we wake up the next morning."

Carrie turned as white as a sheet. She said, "But then, if one of us gets hurt, or even killed, does that mean we will be hurt or dead the next morning?"

"It sure looks like it, Sis," I said, "which means we need to do two things. Number one, we need to ask the conductor if we are right on this. And if we are, it means that the second thing we have to do is be careful–very, very careful!"

Chapter Fourteen

It was hard to go to sleep that night, but we knew we needed to. We had to speak to the conductor; we had to know. I lay there tossing and turning, waiting for sleep to come, and as so often happens, it came without me even realizing it.

"Warner Children, board the train at once! The night is waning fast, and you must hurry."

We shot straight up and found ourselves once again in the broad daylight of the early morning at the old train depot. In a flash we were aboard the train once more.

"You have done well on your first two nights. You have three nights left to find him, or it will be too late."

Then he turned his attention to the controls, and the train once more began to clickety-clack down the track slowly, then a bit more quickly, then a bit more, until finally it was chugging along at full speed.

When it was up to speed, I walked up beside the conductor and said, "Sir, we need to ask you something. I broke my watch in the mine last night, but when we woke up in our own day, it was still broken."

"And you want to know," he said with a grim smile from under his too-long mustache, "whether or not the same thing applies to you. If you get hurt or even killed while trying to help the boy will you be hurt or even dead the next morning in your own beds?"

"Yes, Sir," I said. "That's exactly what we need to know."

"Let me ask you a question," he replied after a few seconds of silence. "Will it make a difference in what you do? If you find out that you are actually risking injury or even death, will you choose not to continue trying to help the boy?"

"Sir," Carrie piped in, "do we even have that option? You came to us and asked us to get on board the train, and then you came again last night. Are we even allowed to say no?"

"Young Lady," he said sternly, "you are always allowed to say no. The Lord never forces anyone to serve Him. If you choose to end your involvement, you may say so at any time, and you will find yourself back on this same train taking you back to your beds and your parents. But be warned; if you do so, there will be no one else to do the particular job you have been called to do in the limited time still available. Furthermore, you will not be called upon again for any other of these night-time tasks. You will be allowed to live out your lives as normal kids, then as normal adults, and you will never hear the call in the night from the conductor again. So my question to you is, are you willing to risk everything for someone that does not even know you?"

There was far less time of silence than you might expect before he had his answer. We kids had been taught well by our parents and our pastor. It was Aly that quickly answered for all of us.

"Sir, we three know Someone Who sacrificed everything for us, when we did not know Him. His name is Jesus, and when we were yet sinners He died for us. He has called every believer in Him to follow His example and that includes giving ourselves for others. Our parents have lived that example in front of us, giving of themselves time after time to people hurting or in need. Our pastor once spent a week a thousand miles away from his family with people whose dad had been in a wreck and ended up in a hospital up north. We have been taught better than to walk away just because something may be uncomfortable for us or even dangerous. If this is the task that God has called for us to do, then keep this train running straight, because we Warner children don't back down."

"Good, very good," he said with a smile, "that is exactly what I hoped for and expected, and that is one more reason why you were chosen. And now, I will answer your question. The answer is yes. If you get hurt or even killed in this or any other of the night-time tasks the Master has laid out for you, it will indeed be very real for you the next morning. So, Warner Children, be careful, be very careful."

A few moments later, we were back in the mining town of Callows, in the very early morning hours. The first thing we had to do was go quickly back to the company store, so I could get a new head lamp. Once that was done, we went back up to the church where Mrs. Sarah was waiting for us.

"What news, Children?" she said as we walked in and she leaped up from the altar.

"We haven't found him yet," I said, "but I think we are on the right track. I searched maybe a third of the mine last night and have eliminated it. Carrie found out that the mine boss is looking to incite the war between the miners and the government forces, apparently so he can be named as the new owner of the mine. We believe that your son's disappearance has something to do with that; we just need to find out what it is and where he is."

"What do you need from me?" she asked.

I had already thought of that, and the answer made me shiver a little bit. Quickly, I explained our plans for the day. I was obviously going back into the mine and would, as last night, stay in an extra three hours to search.

Once again, I would need a distraction to help me get out. I looked over at Aly, and she just grinned that mischievous grin of hers. Somehow I got the feeling that a couple more mine guards were going to be having a very rough night.

The tricky part, though, would be for Mrs. Sarah and the girls. I explained that I needed Mrs. Sarah to point out which house belonged to the mine boss. I needed her to get Mrs. McBride out of it somehow, and I needed Carrie and Aly to get in and snoop. If they could find some evidence of what her husband was planning, it may accomplish two things. Number one, it could allow cooler heads to prevail, stop a needless war, and save a lot of bloodshed. Number two, it may be something that we could use as leverage to get Jonathan out of this mess safely.

"Uh, Bro," said Carrie as she pulled me off to the side and whispered in my ear, "I have a question. I am pretty sure that breaking and entering is still illegal in the year 1912. So what happens if we get arrested here in this dream/not a dream? We know that if we get hurt or killed that carries over into our time, but what about getting arrested? Would we even make it back to our time or would we be stuck in 1912 forever, leaving our parents to wonder where we disappeared to during the night?"

"Sis, don't worry," I said "if you do get arrested and stuck in 1912, remember that it could be worse. It could be me." I got that one from my dad, and Carrie gave me the same *Oh no you di-unt!* look that she always gives him when he says something like that.

A few minutes later I was heading up to the mine entrance, falling in with the same weary looking group of men as yesterday.

Chapter Fifteen

Since Kyle was in the mine again that day, I'll pick the story up and tell you what went on on the outside. This is Aly, by the way.

It wasn't any trouble for Mrs. Sarah to show us the McBride's house. While the mine boss was not wealthy like the mine owner, he was at least paid a better salary than the miners themselves. And the McBrides seem to like to flaunt that fact. Their home in the little mining village, nestled up against the trees on the hill, was nicer than the rest of the miner's shanties. It was also painted, brightly painted. It was a peach type of a color, which made it stand out like a sore thumb as far as I was concerned.

As we meandered around outside, Mrs. Sarah seemed lost in thought. I knew she was trying to find a way to get the Missus out of her comfy home long enough for Carrie and I to go in and go through it. Finally, I could see her face light up, and I heard her say as if to no one nearby, "Why yes, thank you Lord, that will do nicely."

Carrie and I looked at her and when she finally turned to us Carrie said, "You seem to have an answer, Mrs. Sarah, what is it?"

"Why Children, it's as plain as Scripture itself. Proverbs 16:18 says, 'Pride goeth before destruction, and an haughty spirit before a fall.' If there is one thing I know about Lou-Ann McBride, it is that she is intensely proud. We shall use that pride to help her to fall today."

With that, Mrs. Sarah strode up to the Peach Palace, as I had nicknamed it, and knocked right on the door. Within just a few seconds, the door opened and the snotty woman herself stepped out onto the porch. She was wearing a fine dress with way too much crinoline. She looked up and down at Mrs. Sarah, positively sneered at her and said in a voice dripping with haughtiness, "Why are you knocking on my door? Rabble isn't tolerated on these premises, and whoever you are, you fit that description."

I could have knocked her teeth out, if I could have reached that high. I take after my grandmothers on both sides, meaning that I am "vertically challenged." I settled for a strong desire to kick her in the kneecap.

"Oh, Mrs. McBride," I heard Mrs. Sarah say in a trembling voice, "I'm so sorry to bother you, Ma'am, but I just didn't know where else to turn. I am just so sick of all the talk and gossip about you, as fine as you are, I just feel like you deserve better."

You should have seen that woman's face turn red! She looked like a nuclear reactor about to blow its lid!

"Gossip! About me?!? Why, who dares, who would ever, oh, I am so mad I could just...Theresa! It's that awful Theresa Tate, isn't it! Now this is just the last straw! I'm a goin' over there right now and give that woman a piece of my mind!"

And with that, she stormed off like an angry tornado, heading towards the other side of the little town.

In a flash Carrie and I were inside the house, which she left unlocked in her haste to give some woman a piece of her very tiny mind. We figured we had a bit of time since there was about to be an extended cat-fight, but we didn't want to take any chances. We knew we were looking for some kind of evidence linking the mine boss to someone in the government and an attempt to cause a war so he could end up as the owner of the mine. We were also hoping for some clue as to the whereabouts of a missing eleven-year-old boy who seemed to be at the center of it all.

Mrs. Sarah was still just meandering around out front. She would act as a sentinel for us, alerting us if the wicked witch started heading back our way or if she was sending any of her flying monkeys after us. My dad had a saying about people like her: "Someone should have dropped a house on that woman and taken

91

her ruby slippers years ago."

We searched from room to room, in drawers (full of random junk, just like drawers in our day), closets (a few men's clothing items, and a bunch of women's clothes, including what appeared to be a number of girdles. Looks like Mrs. Perfect needed some help achieving her look), and then we arrived in the study. There were books on the shelves, many of which obviously had not been touched for years. They were clearly there for show. But it was the desk in the corner that caught my eye. While Carrie was busy rummaging through books, looking for incriminating letters to fall out, I went to the desk. I remembered reading an Agatha Christie story from many years ago, about a letter being hidden in plain sight. So I opened the desk drawers, started working my way through them and within just a few minutes, Bam! Pay dirt!

"Carrie, come here, quick!" I said. She put the book in her hands back on the shelf and ran over to me.

"What is it?" she said. For answer, I held up an envelope, with the name and address of the mine boss in the center. In the upper right hand corner was an eight-cent stamp bearing the likeness of President William Howard Taft. And there, in the upper left hand corner, was the sender:

U.S. GOVERNMENT MAIL
DO NOT TAMPER

Well, we were already guilty of breaking and entering, though I suppose that we didn't really break; we just entered, so we might as well tamper with the mail as well. Quickly but carefully we opened it, unfolded it, and read what it said:

Mr. McBride,

I received your previous correspondence. Your terms are acceptable to us. The assemblage in question will arrive Friday, May 5. A list will follow containing the names of the men we have placed in the mine as workers. They will start things moving. Accompanying the list will be the deed.

"Yes!" I shouted quietly. "We got him!"

"No," Carrie said "we don't, not yet. That letter is only half of what we need. You and I have a pretty good idea what it means, but no one else will. It is all very general, very circumstantial, and can be explained away. No names are given, not even the name of the sender. A deed is mentioned, but what deed? We know it is the deed to the mine, but we can't prove it. We know there are government workers planted in the mine pretending to be miners, ready to start a war and then fade into the background, but we don't know who they are. There is nothing here we can nail this guy with. But what is here is a clear indication of what we need; we need that list and that deed!"

Quickly, we went back to work searching. We did not leave any envelope unopened or any paper unread. After a half an hour, we had to conclude that what we were looking for was simply not in that house!

A whistle! There was someone whistling outside, and in a split second we realized that is was Mrs. Sarah. The Crinoline Cat-Woman must be on her way back!

There have been a few times at home where we girls nearly got into a lot of trouble. It normally goes something like this: Mom or Dad will tell us to clean our room, and we get busy doing other "important stuff" like playing. A kid should never do that, it is just wrong. But anyway, sometimes Mom or Dad would suddenly appear in our door way after having told us to clean and realize that we haven't done it. They will then calmly say, "I am setting the timer for two minutes. If the room is not clean when the timer goes off, the board of education is going to meet with the seat of understanding." The next two minutes look like two Tazmanian devils blurring around the room at top speed, reorganizing and straightening every little thing just perfectly.

We did that now, racing to get every paper and pencil back in its proper spot, except for the fact that the envelope from the government to the mine boss was now empty. We got it done, started to bolt out the front door, and realized in horror that our little Jezebel was coming up the walk way! We turned and raced for the back of the house, opened a window, and piled out of it. Then we pressed ourselves firmly up against the house, covered our mouths with our hands to keep from gasping for air, and sat perfectly still.

We could hear Mrs. McBride stomping around in the house, still as mad as an old wet hen. Then the open window slammed shut, and we nearly jumped out of our skin! A few minutes later we carefully sneaked away through the trees to meet back up with Mrs. Sarah in the little church on the hill. Tucked in my pocket was the letter. Now, we just had to hope and pray that Kyle could get the rest of what we needed in time.

Chapter Sixteen

The work in the mine hadn't gotten any easier since yesterday. My back was aching, my arms felt like wet noodles, and my mind was racing. We had to find that boy, and we had to stay safe doing it. I couldn't let him go without help, but I couldn't let my sisters get hurt either. A brother ought to always look out for his sisters, even if they think they don't need it.

The morning passed with one shovel-full of coal after another. I was going to make some dishonest miner happy yet again today. Finally it was lunch time, and I sat down with my aching back against the dark wall of the mine. A few large footsteps later, big Jackson sat down beside me.

"So, Boy, how is the rescue going?"

"So-so," I said. "I eliminated a third of the mine last night, I intend to do the same again tonight."

"A third of the mine? Really? Lower level and all?"

Have you ever had that heart-sinking feeling? I had it right then. "Lower level? What lower level?"

Jackson chuckled softly and said, "Boy, you really have no idea, do you? This mine is huge. The level you are on is just one part of it. The center corridor eventually drops into an even lower level, an older level, which is not nearly as well organized as this one. I've never worked that level, but they say that it actually has both the man-made mine shafts and some natural caverns. I heard tell once that some people hid out there during the War Between the States. If a boy is either hiding in the mine or being hidden in the mine, it's probably down on that level.

My head dropped, and my hopes along with it. If the mine was that big, and if the lower level that unorganized, my chances of finding him in time had just gone from slim to none.

"Relax, Boy," said the big man beside me, as if reading my thoughts. "The Good Book says that with God, nothing shall be impossible."

He was right. So then and there I prayed a quick prayer and asked God to forgive me for doubting. I made up my mind that that very night I would head down to the lower level, continue my search, and count on God to show me the way.

The rest of our short lunch we spent talking about different things, mostly about Jackson himself. I learned that he was a widower, his wife having died just a couple of years ago of Tuberculosis. They had not had any children. He had been a Christian for ten years now, having gotten saved at a brush arbor meeting held by a circuit riding preacher. The town of Callows had been his home for just over a year, he had moved there from another part of West Virginia. He seemed to still have a sadness in his heart missing his wife; he sort of sounded like he was tearing up as he talked about her.

After lunch, it was back to the work. The next six hours were more of the same back-breaking, muscle-aching labor: pick-pick-shovel, pick-pick-shovel. Finally, I looked down at Carrie's watch, which she had let me borrow (which, by the way, was humiliating. How many guys have to wear a pink banded rhinestone watch?) and saw that it was just moments from quitting time. I watched for just the right moment, and when I was sure no one was watching, I quickly doused my head lamp and dove under the coal ledge I had been working on. Just like the night before, I lay there totally quite, until I was sure everyone was gone from the mine. Then I crawled out, re-lit my head lamp, and sprinted (much more carefully than last night) towards the center corridor. I hit the corridor, turned right, and sprinted for what must have been two miles, until the ground almost unexpectedly dropped sharply away from me. This had to be the entrance to the lower level that Jackson had spoken of.

I looked at the watch and saw that between hiding till everyone left the mine and running to my present location, I had about two hours and fifteen minutes to search and then get back to the entrance of the mine in time for whatever distraction the girls had planned for tonight.

This time my searching would be a little easier. I had concealed a small LED flashlight in my pocket at bedtime and brought it with me. I clicked it on, and compared to the head lamp, it lit the place up like Christmas. Quickly I jogged down to the lower level and took time to get my bearings.

This place really was massive! It was clearly a very old section of the mine, one that ran together with what were obviously natural underground caves. I wondered what the first man that ever dug into that section and looked around must have thought. Whoever he was, he would have been the first person since the creation of earth to look on that place.

I knew that even with my reasonably good sense of direction, it would be easy to get turned around in a place like this. I couldn't afford to get lost for even a minute, I might not make it back out in time. I wished I had some chalk with me to mark the walls, but I quickly dismissed that idea. Even if I had had the chalk, marks like that would be easily seen by miners and mine bosses and would arouse a lot of suspicion.

Somehow, every smart idea I ever had seemed to always be a "dad thing." Standing there considering my problem, I remembered my dad and I hiking on some of our two and three day trips through different wilderness areas. My dad would often stop and point out different markings along the way. Often, we would see a little triangle of rocks sitting on one side of a fork in a trail. Dad would point out to me that that meant to go that way, instead of the other. Using that technique here in the coal mine would be easy. Bits of coal were laying everywhere, and piling a few of them up would never be anything that anyone noticed unless they were actually looking for it.

That began my search of the large cavern on the lower level. Using my LED light, I was able to search a much larger area much quicker than I had searched last night. The area was huge, but the light went a long way. Within just a little while I had covered a massive area and still had nothing. I was getting so frustrated; I should have had something by now! I sat down for just a moment beside a new little corridor going down towards the right and put my head in my hands to pray and to think. And during that prayer, I heard a voice.

Chapter Seventeen

It wasn't the voice of the Lord I heard; you already know that. God speaks to your heart when you pray but not to your ears. No, the voice I heard was a human voice! It was coming from that corridor going down to the right and seemed to be a long way off. There was no good reason for anyone to be in the mine at night, especially on this low level. The only two reasons I could think of for anyone being in there after hours was either to find or to hide a little boy. Quickly I was on my feet. I covered my LED light with my shirt tail, to make it give out just a very low light. Then I crept along the passage, going down, down, down, listening to the voice.

It soon occurred to me that it was not *a* voice but a few voices. The voices of men– gruff and angry voices. I continued to ease down the corridor toward those voices. Suddenly, I noticed light up ahead. Getting

103

down on my belly and easing ever forward, I finally came to the entrance of a large, cavernous room. It looked like something that had been made that way since the dawn of time. I eased my head around the corner, being careful to stay unseen and unheard. Within seconds I was able to survey and evaluate the room and the situation. In the middle of the room was a table; around the edge of the room were lights. Sitting around that table were four men, facing the back wall. In the middle of the back wall was a very, very narrow crevasse that ran from floor to ceiling. The men were staring at that crevasse, talking to it.

"Aren't you about tired of this, Boy?" said the rough looking man at the right side of the table. "We've been at this for five nights now. Why don't you just come on out, give us the papers, and we can all forget about this and go home?"

Then a scared sounding voice from inside the crevasse spoke back. "You're all too big to get in, so just go away!"

"But you're too small to get past us if you come out," laughed a filthy man on the left. "And you've been without water for five days now. Within another day or two, you're going to die in there anyway, and those precious papers in your hand won't matter."

"I know what you're doing; I overheard the mine boss talking about it! You won't get away with it!" replied the little voice.

"So you snatched the papers right out of

his hand and ran like a scared rabbit," said a big man in the center. "And where has that gotten you? You're stuck in a hole inside a mountain, how big is it back there past this crevasse, four or five feet at most? You can't get out, the coal war is going to happen, the owner is going to lose the mine, and most likely go to jail once we put the blame on him for being behind the shooting that starts the war. Those papers you are holding will never see the light of day, and you're going to die all alone. Does that sound like a good plan to you?"

I could hear sniffling and soft crying coming from inside that tiny crevasse. I now knew that a little boy had done a very brave thing and that it was costing him dearly. I could also tell that he was getting scared, tired, and thirsty and was about to give up. If he did a lot of men would die, and a bad guy would get away with stealing a mine. I had to do something, fast, but there were four grown men between me and that little boy, and I only had a few minutes to get back to the mine's entrance. My mind raced furiously. Then it hit me. It was a very long shot, but it just might work. I quietly backed a few dozen yards back up the shaft, where I knew my light would not be seen. Then I clicked it on and grabbed my little New Testament that I carried everywhere out of a pocket. I really, really hated to do this, but I quickly tore a page out of the front section, grabbed a tiny piece of coal and scrawled a note on it. It said, "Hang on, help is on the way."

Then I wrapped that note around my head lamp, where he would be able to use it to see, and tied it up tight with part of a lace from my left work boot. Then I eased back down to the entrance of the room.

My dad has a great arm. I do too. But the difference between him and me has always been accuracy. If my dad throws at something, he hits it. But my throws are way less dependable, sometimes sailing wide right, sometimes wide left. I couldn't let that happen this time or all was definitely lost. Even if I hit the throw just right, I knew that it was going to be a massive sprint back to the entrance. If I didn't get there with a huge lead and if the distraction was not right on time, I was doomed. A lot could sure go wrong with this plan, and my every move would have to be perfect for anything to even have a chance of going right!

Praying, praying hard, I watched for just the right moment. Then I stood up, stepped quickly out, and fired my package towards that crevasse with all my might. Then I turned and ran like a deer in hunting season.

Chapter Eighteen

I wouldn't find out till later but two very good things happened. One, the throw was perfect. It sailed dead-center through the crevasse. And two, the men stood there arguing over what had just happened. They all heard something whoosh over their heads, and they all heard the clattering as the package landed in the little room past the crevasse, but none of them had any clue what it was or where it came from. One of them suggested that someone had been in there and thrown something past them, but the others argued him out of what was the only logical position. It was as if the Lord had fulfilled a real cool passage of Scripture. Psalm 35:4 says "Let them be confounded and put to shame that seek after my soul: let them be turned back and brought to confusion that devise my hurt."

All I can figure is that God confounded and confused those wicked men, otherwise they surely would have known what just happened.

But I didn't know any of that at the time. At the time, I was sure that all of the demons and devils of Hell were right on my heels, chasing me down. I am sure that I ran the best race of my life getting back to the entrance of that mine!

Finally, panting, gasping, I pulled up a hundred yards or so short of the entrance and listened. All I could hear was my heart and lungs pounding. An elephant could have been blaring at me from a foot away, and I would have had trouble hearing him right then. Finally, everything quieted down in me, and I was able to listen and hear. I could not hear the sound of pursuit; that was good. I walked 90 of the last hundred yards toward the mine entrance, then belly-crawled the last ten yards and looked over the edge. Sure enough, there were two men standing guard, and they were the same two men from last night! They looked as jumpy as a long-tailed cat in a room full of rocking chairs. I only had to wait a minute for the fun to start. Yet once again, when it came, it surprised even me.

"Thwap–thwap, thwap–thwap– thwap!"

I had to hold my mouth yet again to keep from laughing; I knew the sound of those "thwaps." That was the sound of the paint-ball guns that we carry with us everywhere we go! I watched those two men nearly jump out of their skin. Then I saw when they turned towards each other, and in the light of the lamps by the mine's entrance, I could see big red spots, two on the chest of one, three on the other. You know it was paint from a paint ball gun. My sisters knew that it was paint from a paint ball gun. I knew that it was paint from a paint ball gun. But as far as those two already scared men knew, they were bleeding, having been shot by some strange new weapon, probably controlled by whatever being possessed the power of the evil red dot! I tell you, those men screamed like little girls as they went running and crashing through the trees, I'm guessing never to be heard from again.

Carrie and Aly came running, laughing, and I ran out to meet them. Then we all headed for the sleep spot, taking time to fill each other in along the way on what we had learned.

Chapter Nineteen

We woke once again to the sound of the droning of the air conditioner in the Prophet's Chamber. Before going to sleep under the stars back in our dream/not a dream, we had compared notes. We now had a pretty decent idea of what was going on. Carrie still had the intentionally vague note taken from the McBride house. We figure that, combined with whatever papers Jonathan had snatched and was holding with him underneath that mountain, there was enough evidence to stop the coming bloodshed and keep the mine from being stolen. Now we just had to find a way to rescue that little boy and get those papers in his hand to whatever authorities weren't part of the conspiracy!

That obviously presented a bit of a problem. Not just the part about how to get him out past the four men guarding him but also knowing who to trust with the evidence. As we lay there awake in the early morning at the Prophet's Chamber, stretching and yawning, we knew we had a maximum of two more days or nights, depending on perspective, to get the job done. My heart ached for a scared, hungry, thirsty little boy hiding behind an impossibly narrow crevasse deep in a mountain. I hoped, I prayed, that my throw had been true and that he had been able to light my head lamp and read the note.

Breakfast that morning was good. We had home-made biscuits with egg and tomato slices. Buddy, I love me some tomato! I could survive an entire summer on tomato and mayonnaise sandwiches. As we sat there silently scarfing our biscuits down, Pastor Neeson and our mom and dad laid out the plans for the day. This was going to be a bit of a free day. The pastor had some work to do around the church. So we would entertain ourselves, which we are good at, and then meet him and his family in town for lunch.

We ran down into Montgomery after breakfast. We explored the town in short order, then we headed back out of town and rode up a mountain road through several tiny towns. One of those towns was called Deep Water. Once we got over the mountain it did not take us long to figure out that there was nothing on that side of the mountain either. So we turned around and came back. On the way back over the mountain, we came around a curve and saw that traffic was stopped in both directions. Right across the road on which we had just driven five minutes earlier, a huge power pole had cracked at the bottom and crashed across both lanes. If it had landed on anyone, they would have been killed. People need to remember how fragile life is and make sure they are saved! Dad and I helped some folks get it out of the road and went on our way.

We came back down into town and then went to the adjacent town (metropolis) of Smithers. We did find a sort of Christian Bookstore there. Officially it is a Christian bookstore but it is also a JC Penny's mail order place, complete with JC Penney's magazines. We did find some cool things there. They had some 80% off books that we got for the church bookstore back home. But the best part was the cat...

They have a cat in that store that looks like a miniature Bengal Tiger. It is, in fact, called a Bengal! It has a pelt more so than typical cat fur. That is the silkiest cat I have ever seen or petted. But it is also about half dog; the owner took a metal spoon and slid it across the floor, and the cat went and chased it and brought it back! We had a ball playing fetch with that cat for the next little while. It is a $500 cat, and the owner says it is not even "show quality."

From there we went driving again, up a mountain road on the other side, up past Connelton. We found a dirt road/pathway coming off the road, and we went four wheeling in the Yukon! Way cool! And just like my dad to do something like that. We came back into Montgomery, met the pastor and his family at the Mexican Restaurant and had great food and fellowship.

From there it was back to the church. Dad and the pastor then went out and did some visiting, and they came back rejoicing that a 70-year-old lady had been won to the Lord.

Service was good once again; those people are really sweet and love to worship. Then it was back into town for ice cream and fellowship once more and right back to the Prophet's Chamber so we could get some sleep.

In the few minutes before lights out, Carrie and Aly and I lay there talking, thinking out loud, planning. We still had no good answer as to how to get the boy out safely or who to give the evidence to that could be trusted. We whispered and planned and schemed and thought, and somewhere in the midst of it all we fell asleep.

Chapter Twenty

"Warner Children, come quickly!"

By now we all knew the drill very well and were up and into the train like we had been shot out of a cannon. The train reached and grabbed for the inches and feet ahead of it, picking up more and more momentum with each passing moment. Soon we were flying down the tracks once more, heading for the little town of Callows, hopefully to rescue a little boy in danger.

The conductor kept his eyes ahead on the tracks and said nothing. So I slid up beside him and began the conversation.

"How are we doing so far?"

"You have accomplished much," he said "but time is short. You still have two unanswered questions in your minds, so I would use this time that we are traveling to think and pray if I were you."

And so we did. It was a silent trip while

the conductor conducted and the would-be rescuers sat thinking and praying. Soon we were at our destination out on the street and making our way back up to the little church to rendezvous with Mrs. Sarah. We walked in, and in a panic, saw her lying across the altar, passed out!

As we rushed up to her and knelt down to reach her, her eyes opened, and we realized that she had been asleep.

"I'm sorry, Children," she said. "I didn't mean to startle you. I stayed here all night and prayed, and I guess I just fell asleep. You three are taking such risks for me and my son, and I just felt like the least I could do was get hold of the altar of God and pray for His protection upon you and for Him to give you wisdom."

"We thank you, Mrs. Sarah," I said, "and we surely do need both. But we also need you to stay healthy and alert for when we do get your son. And now, if you will kindly sit down on the front pew, I will tell you what we have learned and what we are planning."

I truly felt sorry for that dear young mother. She positively wept when we told her about her son–great, heaving sobs until it seemed she would stop breathing altogether. I knew that she was both relieved to learn that he was alive and anguished over the danger that he was in.

"That is just Jonathan up one side and down the other," she said while brushing away a tear. "He is quick to think, quick to react, and wants right to prevail more than anything in this world. I can easily see him snatching those papers and running. And I just praise the good God of Heaven that He made a place, a cleft in the rock for my boy to hide in."

She sniffed once or twice, wiped away a few more tears, and then reached for the Bible on the altar. It was old, very old, and had obviously been read and prayed over and preached from for many a year. She opened that precious old Book and flipped it open to Psalm 94:22. She seemed to get a faraway look in her eyes as she read aloud, "But the LORD is my defence; and my God is the rock of my refuge."

And then, as if she had ceased to be aware of our presence, she knelt back down by the altar and prayed. "Lord, I thank Thee that Thou art my Defense, my Rock, my Refuge, and that of my son as well. Lord, You have given me this precious child, and You have provided for him a place to run to. You have hidden him in the rock as You did the Psalmist of old. Dear Lord, I plead for Your continued protection upon him. Bring to nought the counsels of wicked men. May those that have sought to do wrong be snared in the net that they themselves have laid..."

She continued to pray, pouring out her heart to the Lord. I felt as if I was standing on holy ground, and I could tell from looking at Little Sis and Littler Sis that they felt the same way. Together, without any spoken word between us, we all eased out quietly and left a

117

mother to pray.

Once we were outside, we laid out what little plans we had. On one part, I had received an answer. I still didn't know how to get the boy out safely, but I believed I knew who to turn to if we could.

"Sis," I said to them both, "I have an idea. We are here in 1912; we know that there are some corrupt mine officials and some corrupt government officials, and we don't know which ones are which. We have no idea who on either side can be trusted. But there is someone that I am willing to take a chance on trusting, someone we should have thought of days ago."

Quickly I explained to them what I needed, then they were off in a flash one direction, and I was off in a flash towards the mine. I was determined to end this thing today. Why go five days when you can finish in four? Dad always preaches for us to be early, and this was as good a time as ever to put that into practice. Besides, if this all fell through today, we would still have 24 hours to say our goodbyes before we were locked up forever a century before our time.

Chapter Twenty-one

That day of work in the mine seemed to drag on forever. Worse, big Jackson was not there. I didn't know if he was sick that day or had been fired, but for whatever reason, my one friend in the mine was gone. I spent the morning pick-pick-shoveling, pick-pick-shoveling, and finally stopped to sit beside the wall and eat my lunch. I could be good at this mine work, I thought, but I would sure rather end up with a career that let me see the light of day!

The hours after lunch seemed to drag by even more slowly than the morning had. And as they passed, I could feel a tightness growing in my chest. I knew that it was nerves because I still had no idea how to win the battle that lay ahead. I thought, I prayed, I cried out to God, but I could not seem to get any answer in my mind as to how to get a scared little boy past four grown men trying to keep him in. The hours passed away, I dove under my coal ledge, and yet laying there in the darkness, there was still no answer. And then from somewhere, a memory verse came to my mind:

Mark 13:11 "But when they shall lead you, and deliver you up, take no thought beforehand what ye shall speak, neither do ye premeditate: but whatsoever shall be given you in that hour, that speak ye: for it is not ye that speak, but the Holy Ghost."

Now why, why should that particular verse occur to mind at a time like this? I would have hoped for a verse giving me some brilliant plan, but instead, God impressed upon my heart a verse that seemed to tell me not to plan at all! That is not what I wanted to hear. I actually lay there under that ledge, arguing with the Lord over that concept. But He quickly put me in my place with yet another verse:

Proverbs 3:5-6 "Trust in the LORD with all thine heart; and lean not unto thine own understanding. In all thy ways acknowledge him, and he shall direct thy paths."

I knew that it was pointless to argue. It made no sense to me, but if God wanted me to simply march into that room on the lower level and announce that I was there to take the boy, all I could do was just do it!

This, I thought as I clicked on my LED light and walked that way, *is going to be the worst rescue attempt in the history of mankind.* Then I broke into a jog and in a short time was at my destination. Once again I got down on my belly, crawled up to the edge of the room, and looked around the corner. Once again on this night I could see the same four men guarding the same tiny crevasse in the mountain. They seemed almost giddy as they verbally tormented the scared little boy who was just out of their reach.

"Hey, Boy!" said a large man with a pot-belly, "are you gettin' hungry in there? You been what, six days without food and water? See if you can smell my breath, Boy," then he breathed really hard into that split in the rock. "That's the smell of apple pie, and my, my, my, was it good! I think I'll have another slice out here while you're in there." Then he laughed a coarse laugh and uttered a string of curse words at the brave little boy in the rock.

And then he made one last mistake. "And by the way, Boy, we now know who your mama is. And when we leave here tonight I'm a goin' by to pay sweet Sarah a little visit. Don't you think she'd like a big ol' kiss from Big Bubba? Hah, Hah, Hah, I bet she would! Yes, Sir, Boy, me and your mama are gonna have ourselves a good old time, and who do you think can stop me?"

"I can."

I heard myself say the words and realized that I had stepped out into the open. I was mad. Really mad. Furious may even be a better description. I thought of my own mom, and then of sweet Mrs. Sarah, and my whole world went red with fury at this overgrown oaf.

121

Now I knew why God wouldn't let me make any plans. They would have all gone out the window anyway at that moment because all I could think of was smashing this jerk's teeth down his face, all three of them. I figured I wasn't going to come out of this alive, but I was mad enough that all I cared about was making sure he didn't either.

Those four men whirled around like a shot when they heard me speak. Then they stood there for a few seconds, dumbfounded, and then...they laughed.

"Well, if there isn't another boy-hero down here in the mine!" said Bubba Bad Breath. "Why don't you just run right on past us and join your little buddy there in his hole in the wall? That way neither of you has to die alone?"

"That isn't my intention," I said while walking towards him. "My intention is to smash your face in and leave here with that brave little guy behind you. Now, why don't we just get right to it; I never have been much for yapping."

Apparently he found that funny because he turned to his buddies on the right of him to laugh and started to say something which I assumed would not be worth hearing. His turning to the side was his mistake, and I made him pay for it. Quickly I closed the gap, fired a prayer upward and a right hook outward. He turned back towards me as it was coming, which made things even better. I made incredibly solid contact with his jaw, I mean it sounded like a gun had gone off! He went down on one knee and then the battle was on. The other three rushed in, and in just a second I was pinned to the wall and watching as one of the other men rared back his fist, intending to smash my face in. I braced myself, knowing I couldn't do a thing about it. His fist started forward...and then stopped in mid air. I blinked involuntarily and then saw a big gloved hand holding that arm, and that big gloved hand was attached to a really big arm, which was attached to my really big friend Jackson, that had appeared out of nowhere just when I needed him most.

Jackson whipped the man's arm around and smashed him in the face with a straight left punch, crumpling him like a sack of potatoes. Then the other two were on him, and it just looked like a blur of punches being given and taken from one good guy and two bad guys.

I didn't have but about a second to watch that, though, when I was back in a battle of my own. Bubba Bad Breath was back on his feet, rubbing his jaw, and he had a raging bull look in his eyes. I knew I had one in my eyes as well, and we would just have to see who was madder. Screaming, the pot-bellied pugilist came rushing in, both hands extended towards my throat. I knew that, as strong as I was, my fourteen-year-old muscles were no match for this big bully. I would have to be both mad and calculated. My dad would call it being "a stone cold killer."

As the big man rushed toward me, arms extended, I turned away from him as if to run, and then lifted my knee in front of me, braced myself against the wall, and threw as hard of a side-kick backwards as I could. My dad is an actual black-belt in Japanese Shotakan Karate, and he has taught me a few simple moves through the years. That side kick landed squarely in the big man's gut. And with him rushing in and me braced against the wall, it was like hitting him in the stomach with a ball bat. I heard all the air rush out of him, and he immediately dropped to his knees, completely and unexpectedly out of breath.

I knew that was not enough, and that I had to press the advantage while I had it. The hardest part of the body is the elbow, and one of the most vulnerable parts of the body is the soft spot at the back of the head where the neck and head join. With the big man bent totally over like that, I had a good chance to put him out. I extended my arm straight and high into the air, and in a rush, brought my elbow down into the back of his head.

I knew when it hit that the lights were going off in his brain, and he was seeing stars. He crumpled to the ground, and I pressed the advantage yet again. I rolled him over, straddled his torso, and began unloading on his face with one straight right punch after another. I fully intended to fulfill my promise of knocking his teeth down his throat. As I ripped into him with one punch after another, suddenly it was my arm that was stopped in mid-air.

"That's enough, Young Man" said my smiling buddy big Jackson. "You've done him in. You're not here to kill anybody; you're here to rescue him," and he turned towards the back wall, where a tired, scared looking little boy was standing.

Chapter Twenty-two

As I surveyed the scene, I could quickly see what had happened. Big Jackson had been more than a match for the three would-be bad men. They were all laying at various places in the room and all looked to be very unconscious and in very bad shape. My man looked the same. Immediately I was just a little disappointed; after all, who was I going to tell?

But the sight that thrilled my heart more than the scene of the victory we had just had, was the sight of a little boy, out in the open, holding some very important papers. He took a step forward...and collapsed. Quickly we went to him. We opened up the lunch pails from the bad-guy miners, and slowly gave him his first food and water for six days. We knew we had to go slowly, or he would get sick.

After a few minutes, he seemed to perk up a bit. In the mean time, while Jackson helped him, I quickly looked over the papers that had been in his hand. I smiled a really big smile, and I knew it would be enough.

We half walked and half carried that precious boy back out of the lower level, up to the higher level, down the main corridor, and to the entrance of the mine. We would not wait for the distraction tonight. I was convinced we could whip the world and was anxious to try. We marched out of the mine, and in unison, two guards turned towards us. Would you believe it? It was the same two guys from the previous two nights that I assumed would never be seen again! As they turned, I said one word very loudly, "BOO!"

They fainted. Both of them.

A second later, Carrie and Aly rushed up to us, clearly a little perturbed.

"What was that?" said Carrie. "You were supposed to wait for us to distract them!"

"Sorry, Sis," I said. "We were just tired of being in that mine."

"But what are we going to do with this Vaseline, box of sparklers, and bottle of Tabasco sauce?" asked Aly with a pout.

I just stared at her blankly for a minute, considering those three items, and could not even begin to fathom what she had had in mind. Somehow, I knew that it would have been absolutely epic.

"Next time, Littlest Sis," I said. "Now, did you get him?"

"We got him," said Carrie. "He is waiting for us at the church."

It took us roughly twenty minutes to cover the ground to the church. We went slowly and carefully, not wanting to be seen by anyone just yet. As we got to the front door of the church, my heart began to soar, anticipating what was coming. A second later we swung the doors open, and Jonathan walked in ahead of us. Within an instant his mother was running for him and he for her, and he was leaping up into her arms saying, "Mother! Mother!" He wasn't a bread winner for the family at that moment; he was just a precious little boy who had been missing his mom. The tears flowed...and Jonathan and his mom cried too. What a reunion! I suspected that it looked a lot like Heaven will look, when each of us who are saved find ourselves on the street of gold, leaping into the arms of moms and dads and grandmas and grandpas that have gone on before us.

We let them hug and cry for a good while, watching Mrs. Sarah stroke the hair of her boy and tell him how much she loved him and had missed him.

Finally, we got them to sit down for just a moment, so we could take care of our last huge problem. I looked toward the pulpit area of the church and caught the smiling face of a man that I did not know but figured I could trust. My dad had taught us since we were little that if we were ever in trouble to find a pastor somewhere to turn to. Those Godly men give their lives to serve others when they could make far more money and be far less despised if they chose another way in life. I didn't know who among the miners or who among the government I could trust, but I knew that a pastor could stand up, lift up his voice, and be heard by everyone.

Quickly we introduced ourselves to him, and he to us. Then we showed him what we had to work with, and it was plenty. Six days earlier little Jonathan had been in the mine working under a ledge and the poor little guy had fallen asleep. When he woke up it was after hours, yet there were voices from men standing just past the ledge. He quickly recognized the voice of Cyril McBride, the mine boss:

> "I have the deed to the mine, dated for seven days from now, already in my name, right here in this packet in my hand. When old man Buchanan gets framed for starting the war, I will go to the register of deeds, file this, and it will be mine. A second letter in the packet is from Colonel Smith. It contains the names of the five men he has planted here in the mine as workers. When the government forces get here Friday night, they will be near the back of the pack of miners as they go out to meet them. They will all pull out guns

and fire into the government lines, then they will retreat into the mine while the miners and the government forces clash. The third letter is a letter implicating Mr. Buchanan as the man behind it all, supposedly written by a co-conspirator. This packet contains everything we need to make us all very wealthy men, Gentlemen."

That brave kid, hearing what was happening, slipped out from under the ledge and impulsively rushed right between those men, snatched the packet, and ran like a scared rabbit. The men gave chase, farther and farther, down one corridor after another, closing in the entire time. Finally, in desperation, the boy had rushed into the big room with the men hot on his tail, and just in the nick of time saw that crevasse in the wall. He rushed for it, turned sideways, and launched himself inside just a split second ahead of many filthy, grasping hands. That had begun a six day ordeal for him.

After two days of sitting there scared in the darkness, he had prayed, "Lord, I'm scared, and mom won't know why I haven't come home and may not ever know. Lord, I need some help. Please God, send somebody to help me."

Unbeknownst to him, in fact, he would never know it, a voice had rung out at that exact moment, 100 years later; "Kyle! Carrie! Aly!"

Chapter Twenty-three

The pastor looked over all of the papers, and he grinned a beautiful grin. "Children," he said, "I am proud of you all. What you have all done was very dangerous, but it will save many lives. It's time we turn the lights on."

I knew what he meant by that. John 3:20 says "For every one that doeth evil hateth the light, neither cometh to the light, lest his deeds should be reproved." Bad people like to keep their deeds hidden. This pastor was about to make sure that could not happen.

A moment later the church bells began to ring–loud, long, over and over and over. The pastor was pulling on that rope with all of his might, and everyone in the valley knew what it meant: "Assemble at the church, there is something going on."

The pastor stopped pulling the rope, took all of the papers, and walked out onto the front porch. It took about fifteen minutes, but the stores, streets, valleys, everything emptied as multiplied hundreds of people gathered around the church. There were only four men that I knew would not be there, they were having a nice long, right-hook induced nap.

Poor people came and gathered. Old people. Young people. Black people and white people and the barber and the clerk from the company store. And right there in front of this multitude of mostly miners, looking very important, was Cyril and Lou-Ann McBride, not having a clue that their plans were unraveling since Jonathan and his mother were hidden out of view inside the church.

"Good people of Callows," began the pastor, "we have an issue to deal with. We would all like to be able to think the best of everyone, but the truth is, not everyone needs to be well thought of. The Scripture makes it clear that many men and many women are in fact wolves. They may wear sheep's clothing, but they are wolves nonetheless."

A murmur was making its way across the crowd. When the pastor gave a warning like this, they knew something was bad wrong, and they were ready to back up God's man in whatever way he needed.

"There are some in the midst who are willing to have innocent blood be shed for their own selfish gain," he continued, and as he did I watched the McBrides begin to squirm and begin to look nervous.

"You all know that there is great tension

134

between the miners and the government. What you do not know is that some who claim to be for the miners are in fact stirring up that trouble, looking to start a war, hoping to end up with possession of the mine once the dust has cleared."

At that point, seeing the trouble that was coming, Cyril McBride interrupted the pastor. That was a mistake.

"Look here, Preacher, you're a bit young to be spouting off about things you don't understand, don't you think?"

I really loved what I saw next. Three men surrounded him, and one of them grabbed him by his fancy lapel and physically lifted him off of the ground. "YOU look here," said the rough miner, "I don't care how much money you have or what position you hold, you will either show some respect to the man of God, or I will teach you myself to have respect for him. Are we clear?"

Ashen white, the mine boss shook his head yes, and the miner set him back down. But several of them then enclosed him in a circle, seeming to sense where the pastor was going with all of this and who would end up being the culprit.

I watched the McBrides as the pastor continued speaking. I could see him leaning over to whisper in her ear, and I could clearly make out the words "no proof." I smiled to myself, and I knew it would look like very mischievous smile. Man, was this guy in for a surprise!

Just a moment later, the pastor produced a packet from inside his coat. When the mine boss saw it, his face fell, and he knew it was all over. The next few minutes were a whirlwind of activity. Both of the McBrides and everyone else involved in the conspiracy were grabbed, tied up tightly, and deposited on the floor of the railroad depot, waiting for a train to come pick them up and take them to Charleston where they would face justice. A telegraph was sent to a man in Washington that the pastor personally knew and trusted. That very night, many government men would also face justice. Colonel Smith would actually later be tried and convicted of treason.

As for us, the night was nearly over, and I figured that our task was almost done. I say almost because there was one last thing I wanted to do. Before we went to our sleep spot to catch our ride back home, I pulled all of our little group together: me and Sis and Sis, Jonathan our rescued kid, his sweet widowed mom Sarah (who could use a good husband), and my friend big Jackson, a widower (who could use a good wife.) And then I smiled at how forward I was about to be...

Coming Soon
Spring 2013

The Night Heroes Book Two
Free Fall

The sensation of jumping out of an airplane is difficult to describe. Everything within you is protesting the idea. God has built a survival instinct into mankind and that very instinct has to be fought against in order to jump out of a plane. We were lined up at the door: me first, then Aly, then Carrie. When the pilot opened the door there was a whooshing sound that filled the cabin and a massive change in air pressure. Once we adjusted to that, I got right up by the door with the other two behind me in a line. The pilot, who would now be our jumpmaster, had his left hand on the top of the door frame, his right arm across the opening, and was looking down at the ground. Then he began to count backwards from five:

"Five...four...three...two...one... Go!"

A jump into nothingness...a split second of falling in which your stomach jumps up into your throat...then a jerk as the static line engages the parachute. After that there were four or five seconds where I was not breathing, but had not yet realized that fact. Finally that breath came, in gasps. Quickly I got myself oriented and looked around for my sisters. Aly was off to my left, Carrie to the right. The plane was quickly getting smaller and smaller as it streaked away from us. Every second brought us a bit closer to the ground and in about 10-12 more of those seconds I knew we would be down. Down on the ground in very dangerous place. Germany of World War II...

Meet the Author

Dr. Wagner is the founder and pastor of Cornerstone Baptist Church of Mooresboro, North Carolina. He was saved in 1979 and began preaching regularly as a twelve year old boy in 1982.

He earned an Associate's Degree in Communications Technology from Cleveland Community College in 1989. He earned his Bachelor's Degree in Pastoral Studies with highest honors in 1997 and then his Master's and Doctorate with highest honors from Carolina Bible College in 2001 and 2003. He founded Cornerstone Baptist Church in 1997. He has been teaching at the Carolina Bible College since 2000 and has been a professor since 2003.

He has been writing books since 2009, with Cry from the Coal Mine being his first fiction book. This book will be part of a series that should include many titles.

Along with pastoring, Dr. Wagner preaches in many revivals, camp meetings, and family conferences each year.

He married Dana in 1994. They have three Children: Caleb, Karis, and Aléthia.